Selected praise for
New York Times and *USA TODAY*
bestselling author
Brenda Jackson

"Brenda Jackson writes romance
that sizzles and characters you fall in love with."
—*New York Times* and *USA TODAY*
bestselling author Lori Foster

"Jackson's trademark ability to weave multiple
characters and side stories together makes
shocking truths all the more exciting."
—*Publishers Weekly*

"Jackson's characters are wonderful, strong,
colorful and hot enough to burn the pages."
—*RT Book Reviews* on *Westmoreland's Way*

"The kind of sizzling, heart-tugging story
Brenda Jackson is famous for."
—*RT Book Reviews* on
Spencer's Forbidden Passion

"This is entertainment at its best."
—*RT Book Reviews* on *Star of His Heart*

Dear Reader,

This is it! The twentieth book in The Westmorelands series and the fifth book about those Denver Westmorelands. For those two reasons alone I knew this book was special from the moment I began writing it.

I always thought of Jason Westmoreland as the quiet storm. Of the three, Derringer, Zane and Jason, Jason was the one who didn't have a lot to say and wouldn't have a lot to say…until it was his time to take center stage. Now, it is his time.

Jason is a man who thinks he knows what he wants, but when he meets Bella Bostwick he isn't so sure anymore. He thinks he would be happy to make Bella an offer, the ultimate proposal, one he thinks she can't refuse. What he doesn't count on is awakening to passion the likes of which he's never had before. And it doesn't take long for him to figure out that Bella is the one woman whose heart he needs to conquer.

I present you with another Westmoreland man who has to come up with a plan to get the woman he wants. That one woman who will make his life complete. It's going to be up to him to prove to Bella that together they can have a forever kind of love.

Happy reading!

Brenda Jackson

BRENDA JACKSON

THE PROPOSAL

Harlequin®

Desire

To Gerald Jackson, Sr. My one and only.

To all my readers who enjoy reading about the Westmorelands,
this book is especially for you!

To my Heavenly Father. How Great Thou Art.

He hath made everything beautiful in his time.
—*Ecclesiastes* 3:11 KJV

ISBN-13: 978-0-373-73102-2

THE PROPOSAL

Copyright © 2011 by Brenda Streater Jackson

Recycling programs
for this product may
not exist in your area.

www.Harlequin.com

Printed in U.S.A.

Selected books by Brenda Jackson

Desire

*Delaney's Desert Sheikh #1473
*A Little Dare #1533
*Thorn's Challenge #1552
*Stone Cold Surrender #1601
*Riding the Storm #1625
*Jared's Counterfeit Fiancée #1654
*The Chase Is On #1690
*The Durango Affair #1727
*Ian's Ultimate Gamble #1756
*Seduction, Westmoreland Style #1778
*Spencer's Forbidden Passion #1838
*Taming Clint Westmoreland #1850
*Cole's Red-Hot Pursuit #1874
*Quade's Babies #1911
*Tall, Dark...Westmoreland! #1928
*Westmoreland's Way #1975
*Hot Westmoreland Nights #2000
*What a Westmoreland Wants #2035
*A Wife for a Westmoreland #2077
*The Proposal #2089

Kimani Arabesque

†Whispered Promises
†Eternally Yours
†One Special Moment
†Fire and Desire
†Secret Love
†True Love
†Surrender
†Sensual Confessions
†Inseparable

Kimani Romance

**Solid Soul #1
**Night Heat #9
**Beyond Temptation #25
**Risky Pleasures #37
**Irresistible Forces #89
**Intimate Seduction #145
**Hidden Pleasures #189

*The Westmorelands
†Madaris Family Saga
**Steele Family titles

BRENDA JACKSON

is a die "heart" romantic who married her childhood sweetheart and still proudly wears the "going steady" ring he gave her when she was fifteen. Because she's always believed in the power of love, Brenda's stories always have happy endings. In her real-life love story, Brenda and her husband of thirty-eight years live in Jacksonville, Florida, and have two sons.

A *New York Times* bestselling author of more than seventy-five romance titles, Brenda is a recent retiree who now divides her time between family, writing and traveling with Gerald. You may write Brenda at P.O. Box 28267, Jacksonville, Florida 32226, by email at WriterBJackson@aol.com or visit her website at www.brendajackson.net.

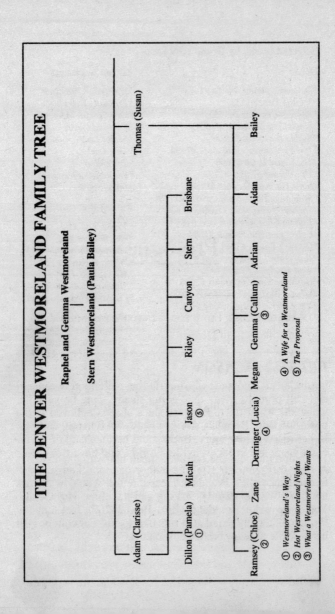

THE DENVER WESTMORELAND FAMILY TREE

Raphel and Gemma Westmoreland

Stern Westmoreland (Paula Bailey)

Adam (Clarisse)   Thomas (Susan)

Dillon (Pamela)   Micah   Jason   Riley   Canyon   Stern   Brisbane   Bailey
①   ⑤

Ramsey (Chloe)   Zane   Derringer (Lucia)   Megan   Gemma (Callum)   Adrian   Aidan
②   ④   ③

① Westmoreland's Way
② Hot Westmoreland Nights
③ What a Westmoreland Wants
④ A Wife for a Westmoreland
⑤ The Proposal

Prologue

"Hello, ma'am, I'm Jason Westmoreland and I'd like to welcome you to Denver."

Even before she turned around, the deep, male voice had Bella Bostwick's stomach clenching as the throaty *sound* vibrated across her skin. And then when she gazed up into his eyes she had to practically force oxygen into her lungs. He had to be the most gorgeous man she'd ever seen.

For a moment she couldn't speak nor was she able to control her gaze from roaming over him and appreciating everything she saw. He was tall, way over six feet, with dark brown eyes, sculpted cheekbones and a chiseled jaw. And then there was his skin, a deep, rich chocolate-brown that had her remembering her craving for that particular treat and how delicious it was. But nothing could be more appealing than his lips and the way they were shaped. Sensuous. Sumptuous. A perfect pair for the sexy smile curving them.

He said he was a Westmoreland and because this charity ball was given on behalf of the Westmoreland Foundation, she could only assume he was one of *those* Westmorelands.

She took the hand he'd extended and wished she hadn't when a heated sizzle rode up her spine the moment she touched it. She tried forcing the sensation away. "And I'm Elizabeth Bostwick, but I prefer just Bella."

The smile curving his lips widened a fraction, enough to send warm blood rushing through her veins. "Hi, Bella."

The way he'd pronounce her name was ultrasexy. She thought his smile was intoxicating and definitely contagious, which was the reason she could so easily return it. "Hi, Jason."

"First, I'd like to offer my condolences on the loss of your grandfather."

"Thank you."

"And then I'm hoping the two of us could talk about the ranch you inherited. If you decide to sell it, I'd like to put in my bid for both the ranch and Hercules."

Bella drew in a deep breath. Her grandfather Herman Bostwick had died last month and left his land and prized stallion to her. She had seen the horse when she'd come to town for the reading of the will and would admit he was beautiful. She had returned to Denver from Savannah only yesterday to handle more legal matters regarding her grandfather's estate. "I haven't decided what I plan on doing regarding the ranch or the livestock, but if I do decide to sell I will keep your interest in mind. But I need to make you aware that according to my uncle Kenneth there are others who've expressed the same interest."

"Yes, I'm sure there are."

He had barely finished his sentence when her uncle suddenly appeared at her side and spoke up. "Westmoreland."

"Mr. Bostwick."

Bella immediately picked up strong negative undercurrents radiating between the two men and the extent of it became rather obvious when her uncle said in a curt tone, "It's time to leave, Bella."

She blinked. "Leave? But we just got here, Uncle Kenneth."

Her uncle smiled down at her as he tucked her arm underneath his. "Yes, dear, but you just arrived in town yesterday and have been quite busy since you've gotten here taking care of business matters."

She arched a brow as she stared at the grand-uncle she only discovered she had a few weeks ago. He hadn't been concerned with how exhausted she was when he'd insisted she accompany him here tonight, saying it was her place to attend this gala in her grandfather's stead.

"Good night, Westmoreland. I'm taking my niece home."

She barely had time to bid Jason farewell when her uncle escorted her to the door. As they proceeded toward the exit she couldn't help glancing over her shoulder to meet Jason's gaze. It was intense and she could tell he hadn't appreciated her uncle's abruptness. And then she saw a smile touch his lips again and she couldn't help reciprocate by smiling back. Was he flirting with her? Was she with him?

"Jason Westmoreland is someone you don't want to get to know, Bella," Kenneth Bostwick said in a gruff tone, apparently noticing the flirtatious exchange between them.

She turned to glance up at her uncle as they walked out into the night. People were still arriving. "Why?"

"He wants Herman's land. None of the Westmorelands are worth knowing. They think they can do whatever the hell they please around these parts." He interrupted her thoughts by saying, "There're a bunch of them and they own a lot of land on the outskirts of town."

She lifted an arched brow. "Near where my grandfather lived?"

"Yes. In fact Jason Westmoreland's land is adjacent to Herman's."

"Really?" She smiled warmly at the thought that Jason Westmoreland lived on property that connected to the land she'd inherited. Technically that made her his neighbor. *No wonder he wants to buy my land,* she thought to herself.

"It's a good thing you're selling Herman's land, but I wouldn't sell it to him under any circumstances."

She frowned when he opened the car for her to get in. "I haven't decided what I plan to do with the ranch, Uncle Kenneth," she reminded him.

He chuckled. "What is there to decide? You know nothing about ranching and a woman of your delicacy, breeding and refinement belongs back in Savannah and not here in Denver trying to run a hundred-acre ranch and enduring harsh winters. Like I told you earlier, I already know someone who wants to buy the ranch along with all the livestock—especially that stallion Hercules. They're offering a lot of money. Just think of all the shoes, dresses and hats you'll be able to buy, not to mention a real nice place near the Atlantic Ocean."

Bella didn't say anything. She figured this was

probably not the time to tell him that as far as she was concerned there was a lot to decide because none of those things he'd mentioned meant anything to her. She refused to make a decision about her inheritance too hastily.

As her uncle's car pulled out of the parking lot, she settled back against the plush leather seats and remembered the exact moment her and Jason Westmoreland's eyes had met.

It was a connection she doubted she would ever forget.

One

One month later

"Did you hear Herman Bostwick's granddaughter is back in Denver and rumor has it she's here to stay?"

Jason Westmoreland's ears perked up on the conversation between his sister-in-law Pam and his two cousins-in-laws Chloe and Lucia. He was at his brother Dillon's house, stretched out on the living room floor playing around with his six-month-old nephew, Denver.

Although the ladies had retired to the dining room to sit at the table and chat, it wasn't hard to hear what they were saying and he thought there was no reason for him not to listen. Especially when the woman they were discussing was a woman who'd captured his attention the moment he'd met her last month at a charity ball. She was a woman he hadn't been able to stop thinking about since.

"Her name is Elizabeth but she goes by Bella," Lucia, who'd recently married his cousin Derringer, was saying. "She came into Dad's paint store the other day and I swear she is simply beautiful. She looks so out of place here in Denver, a real Southern belle amidst a bunch of roughnecks."

"And I hear she intends to run the ranch alone. Her uncle Kenneth has made it known he won't be lifting one finger to help her," Pam said in disgust. "The nerve of the man to be so darn selfish. He was counting on her selling that land to Myers Smith who promised to pay him a bunch of money if the deal went through. It seems everyone would love to get their hands on that land and especially that stallion Hercules."

Including me, Jason thought, as he rolled the ball toward his nephew but kept his ears wide-open. He hadn't known Bella Bostwick had returned to Denver and wondered if she remembered he was interested in purchasing her land and Hercules. He definitely hoped so. His thoughts then shifted to Kenneth Bostwick. The man's attitude didn't surprise him. He'd always acted as if he was entitled, which is probably the reason Kenneth and Herman never got along. And since Herman's death, Kenneth had let it be known around town that he felt the land Bella had inherited should be his. Evidently Herman hadn't seen it that way and had left everything in his will to the granddaughter he'd never met.

"Well, I hope she's cautious as to who she hires to help out on that ranch. I can see a woman that beautiful drawing men in droves, and some will be men who she needs to be leery of," Chloe said.

Jason frowned at the thought of any man drawn to her and didn't fully understand why he reacted that way. Lucia was right in saying Bella was beautiful. He had been totally captivated the moment he'd first seen her. And it had been obvious Kenneth Bostwick hadn't wanted him anywhere near his niece.

Kenneth never liked him and had envied Jason's relationship with old man Herman Bostwick. Most people around these parts had considered Herman mean, ornery and craggy, but Jason was not one of them. He would never forget the one time he had run away from home at eleven and spent the night hidden in Bostwick's barn. The old man had found him the next morning and returned him to his parents. But not before feeding him a tasty breakfast and getting him to help gather eggs from the chickens and milk the cows. It was during that time he'd discovered Herman Bostwick wasn't as mean as everyone thought. In fact, Herman had only been a lonely old man.

Jason had gone back to visit Herman often over the years and had been there the night Hercules had been born. He'd known the moment he'd seen the colt that he would be special. And Herman had even told him that the horse would one day be his. Herman had died in his sleep a few months ago and now his ranch and every single thing on it, including Hercules, belonged to his granddaughter. Everyone assumed she would sell the ranch, but from what he was hearing she had moved to Denver from Savannah.

He hoped to hell she had thought through her decision. Colorado's winters were rough, especially in Denver. And running a spread as big as the one she'd inherited wasn't easy for an experienced rancher; he didn't want to think how it would be for someone who knew nothing about it. Granted if she kept Marvin Allen on as the foreman things might not be so bad, but still, there were a number of ranch hands and some men didn't take kindly to a woman who lacked experience being their boss.

"I think the neighborly thing for us to do is to pay her a visit and welcome her to the area. We can also let her know if there's anything she needs she can call on us," Pam said, interrupting his thoughts.

"I agree," both Lucia and Chloe chimed in.

He couldn't help but agree, as well. Paying his new neighbor a visit and welcoming her to the area was the right thing to do, and he intended to do just that. He might have lost out on a chance to get the ranch but he still wanted Hercules.

But even more than that, he wanted to get to know Bella Bostwick better.

Bella stepped out of the house and onto the porch and looked around at the vast mountains looming before her. The picturesque view almost took her breath away and reminded her of why she had defied her family and moved here from Savannah two weeks ago.

Her overprotective parents had tried talking her out of what they saw as a foolish move on her part mainly because they hadn't wanted her out of their sight. It had been bad enough while growing up when she'd been driven to private schools by a chauffeur each day and trailed everywhere she went by a bodyguard until she was twenty-one.

And the sad thing was that she hadn't known about her grandfather's existence until she was notified of the reading of his will. She hadn't been informed in time to attend the funeral services and a part of her was still upset with her parents for keeping that from her.

She didn't know what happened to put a permanent wedge between father and son, but whatever feud that existed between them should not have included her. She'd had every right to get to know Herman Bostwick and now he was gone. When she thought about the summers she could have spent here visiting him instead of being shipped away to some camp for the summer she couldn't help but feel angry. She used to hate those camps and the snooty kids that usually went to them.

Before leaving Savannah she had reminded her parents that she was twenty-five and old enough to make her own decisions about what she wanted to do with her life. And as far as she was concerned, the trust fund her maternal grandparents had established for her, as well as this ranch she'd now inherited from her paternal grandfather, made living that life a lot easier. It was the first time in her life that she had anything that was truly hers.

It would be too much to ask David and Melissa Bostwick to see things that way and they'd made it perfectly clear that they didn't. She wouldn't be surprised if they were meeting with their attorney at this very moment to come up with a way to force her to return home to Savannah. Well, she had news for them. This was now her home and she intended to stay.

If they'd had anything to say about it she would be in Savannah and getting engaged to marry Hugh Pierce. Although most women would consider Hugh, with his tall, dark and handsome looks and his old-money wealth, a prime catch. And if she really thought hard about it, then she would be one of those women who thought so. But that was the problem. She had to think real hard about it. They'd dated a number of times but there was never any connection, any spark and no real enthusiasm on her part about spending time with him. She had tried as delicately as she could to explain such a thing to her parents but that hadn't stopped them from trying to shove Hugh down her throat every chance they got. That only proved how controlling they could be.

And speaking of controlling...her uncle Kenneth had become another problem. He was her grandfather's fifty-year-old half brother, whom she'd met for the first time when she'd flown in for the reading of the will. He'd assumed the ranch would go to him and had been gravely disappointed that day to discover it hadn't. He had also expected her to sell everything and when she'd made the decision to keep the ranch, he had been furious and said his kindness to her had ended, and that he wouldn't lift a finger to help and wanted her to find out the hard way just what a mistake she had made.

She sank into the porch swing, thinking there was no way she could have made a mistake in deciding to build a life here. She had fallen in love with the land the first time she'd seen it when she'd come for the reading of the will. And it hadn't taken long to decide even though she'd been robbed of the opportunity to connect with her grandfather in life, she would connect with him in death by accepting the gift he'd given her. A part of her felt that although they'd never met, he had somehow known about the miserable childhood she had endured and was giving her the chance to have a way better adult life.

The extra men she had hired to work the ranch so far seemed eager to do so and appreciated the salary she was paying them which, from what she'd heard, was more than fair. She'd always heard if you wanted good people to work for you then you needed to pay them good money.

She was about to get up to go back into the house to pack up more of her grandfather's belongings when she noticed someone on horseback approaching in the distance. She squinted her eyes, remembering this was Denver and people living on the outskirts of town, in the rural sections, often traveled by horseback, and she was grateful for the riding lessons her parents had insisted that she take. She'd always wanted to own a horse and now she had several of them.

As the rider came closer she felt a tingling sensation in the pit if her stomach when she recognized him. Jason Westmoreland. She definitely remembered him from the night of the charity ball and one of the things she remembered the most was his warm smile. She had often wondered if he'd been as ruggedly handsome as she recalled. The closer the rider got she realized he was.

And she had to admit that in the three times she'd been to Denver, he was the closest thing to a modern-day cowboy she had seen. Even now he was riding his horse with an expertise and masculinity that had her heart pounding with every step the horse took. His gaze was steady on her and she couldn't help but stare back. Heat crawled up her spine and waves of sensuous sensations swept through her system. She could feel goose bumps form on her skin. He was definitely the first and only man she'd ever been this attracted to.

She couldn't help wondering why he was paying her a visit. He had expressed interest in her land and in Hercules when she'd met him that night at the charity ball. Was he here to convince her she'd made a mistake in moving here like her parents and uncle had done? Would he try to talk her into selling the land and horse to him? If that was the case then she had the same news for him she'd had for the others. She was staying put and Hercules would remain hers until she decided otherwise.

He brought his horse to a stop at the foot of the porch near a hitching post. "Hello, Bella."

"Jason." She gazed up into the dark brown eyes staring at her and could swear she felt heat radiating from them. The texture of his voice tingled against her skin just as it had that night. "Is there a reason for your visit?"

A smile curved his lips. "I understand you've decided to try your hand at ranching."

She lifted her chin, knowing what was coming next. "That's right. Do you have a problem with it?"

"No, I don't have a problem with it," he said smoothly. "The decision was yours to make. However, I'm sure you know things won't be easy for you."

"Yes, I'm very much aware they won't be. Is there anything else you'd like to say?"

"Yes. We're neighbors and if you ever need my help in any way just let me know."

She blinked. Had he actually offered his help? There had to be a catch and quickly figured what it was. "Is the reason you're being nice that you still want to buy Hercules? If so, you might as well know I haven't made a decision about him yet."

His smile faded and the look on his face suddenly became intense. "The reason I'm being *nice* is that I think of myself as a nice person. And as far as Hercules is concerned, yes, I still want to buy him but that has nothing to do with my offering my help to you as your neighbor."

She knew she had offended him and immediately regretted it. She normally wasn't this mistrusting of people but owning the ranch was a touchy subject with her because so many people were against it. He had wanted the land and Hercules but had accepted her decision and was even offering his help when her own uncle hadn't. Instead of taking it at face value, she'd questioned it. "Maybe I shouldn't have jumped to conclusions."

"Yes, maybe you shouldn't have."

Every cell in her body started to quiver under the intensity of his gaze. At that moment she knew his offer had been sincere. She wasn't sure how she knew; she just did. "I stand corrected. I apologize," she said.

"Apology accepted."

"Thank you." And because she wanted to get back on good footing with him she asked, "How have you been, Jason?"

His features relaxed when he said, "Can't complain." He tilted his Stetson back from his eyes before dismounting from the huge horse as if it was the easiest of things to do.

And neither can I complain, she thought, watching him come up the steps of the porch. There was nothing about seeing him in all his masculine form that any woman could or would complain about. She felt her throat tighten when moments later he was standing in front of her. Something she could recognize as hot, fluid desire closed in on her, making it hard to breathe. Especially when his gaze was holding hers with the same concentration he'd had the night of the ball.

Today in the bright sunlight she was seeing things about him that the lights in the ballroom that night hadn't revealed: the whiteness of his teeth against his dark skin, the thickness of his lashes, the smooth texture of his skin and the broadness of his shoulders beneath his shirt. Another thing she was seeing now as well as what she remembered seeing in full detail that night was the full shape of a pair of sensual lips.

"And what about you, Bella?"

She blinked, realizing he'd spoken. "What about me?" The smile curving his lips returned and in a way that lulled her into thoughts she shouldn't be thinking, like how she'd love kissing that smile on his face.

"How have you been…besides busy?" he asked.

Bella drew in a deep breath and said. "Yes, things have definitely been busy and at times even crazy."

"I bet. And I meant what I said earlier. If you ever need help with anything, let me know."

"Thanks for the offer, I appreciate it." She had seen the turnoff to his ranch. The marker referred to it as Jason's Place. And from what she'd seen through the trees it was a huge ranch and the two-story house was beautiful.

She quickly remembered her manners and said. "I was about to have a cup of tea. Would you like a cup, as well?"

He leaned against the post and his smile widened even more. "Tea?"

"Yes."

She figured he found such a thing amusing if the smile curving his lips was anything to go by. The last thing a cowboy would want after being in the saddle was a cup of tea. A cold beer was probably more to his liking but was the one thing she didn't have in her refrigerator. "I'd understand if you'd rather not," she said.

He chuckled. "A cup of tea is fine."

"You sure?"

He chuckled again. "Yes, I'm positive."

"All right then." She opened the door and he followed her inside.

Beside the fact Jason thought she looked downright beautiful, Bella Bostwick smelled good, as well. He wished there was some way he could ignore the sudden warmth that flowed through his body from her scent streaming through his nostrils.

And then there was the way she was dressed. He had to admit that although she looked downright delectable in her jeans and silk blouse she also looked out of place in them. But as she walked gracefully in front of him, Jason thought that a man could endure a lot of sleepless nights dreaming about a Southern-belle backside shaped like hers.

"If you'll have a seat, Jason, I'll bring the tea right out."

He stopped walking as he realized she must have a pot already made. "All right."

He watched her walk into the kitchen, but instead of taking the seat like she'd offered, he kept standing as he glanced around taking in the changes she'd already made to the place. There were a lot of framed art pieces on the wall, a number of vases filled with flowers, throw rugs on the wood floor and fancy curtains attached to the windows. It was evident that a woman lived here. And she was some woman.

She hadn't hesitated to get her back up when she'd assumed his visit here was less than what he'd told her. He figured Kenneth Bostwick, in addition to no telling how many others, probably hadn't liked her decision not to sell her land and was giving her pure grief about it. He wouldn't be one of those against her decision.

He continued to glance around the room, noting the changes. There were a lot of things that remained the same, like Herman's favorite recliner, but she'd added a spiffy new sofa to go with it. It was just as well. The old one had seen better days. The old man had claimed he would be getting a new one this coming Christmas, not knowing when he'd said it he wouldn't be around.

Jason drew in a deep breath remembering the last time he'd seen Herman Bostwick alive. It had been a month before he'd died. Jason had come to check on him and to ride Hercules. Jason was one of the few people who could do so mainly because he was the one Herman had let break in the horse.

He glanced down to study the patterns on the throw rug beneath his feet thinking how unique looking they were when he heard her reenter the room. He looked up and a part of him wished he hadn't. The short medium brown curls framing her face made her mahogany colored skin appear soft to the touch and perfect for her hazel eyes and high cheekbones.

There was a refinement about her, but he had a feeling she was a force to be reckoned with if she had to be. She'd proven that earlier when she'd assumed he was there to question her sanity about moving here. Maybe he should be questioning his own sanity for not convincing her to move on and return to where she came from. No matter her best intentions, she wasn't cut out to be a rancher, not with her soft hands and manicured nails.

He believed there had to be some inner conflict driving her to try to run the ranch. He decided then and there that he would do whatever he could to help her succeed. And as she set the tea tray down on the table he knew at that moment she was someone he wanted to get to know better in the process.

"It's herbal tea. Do you want me to add any type of sweetener?" she asked.

"No," he said flatly, although he wasn't sure if he did or not. He wasn't a hot tea drinker, but did enjoy a glass of cold sweet tea from time to time. However, for some reason he felt he would probably enjoy his hot tea like he did his coffee—without anything added to it.

"I prefer mine sweet," she said softly, turning and smiling over at him. His guts tightened and he tried like hell to ignore the ache deep within and the attraction for this woman. He'd never felt anything like this before.

He was still standing and when she crossed the room toward him carrying his cup of tea, he had to forcibly propel air through his lungs with every step she took. Her beauty was brutal to the eyes but soothing to the soul, and he was enjoying the view in deep male appreciation. How old was she and what was she doing out here in the middle of nowhere trying to run a ranch?

"Here you are, Jason."

He liked the sound of his name from her lips and when he took the glass from her hands they touched in the process. Immediately, he felt his stomach muscles begin to clench.

"Thanks," he said, thinking he needed to step away from her and not let Bella Bostwick crowd his space. But he also very much wanted to keep her right there. Topping the list was her scent. He wasn't sure what perfume she was wearing but it was definitely an attention grabber, although her beauty alone would do the trick.

"You're welcome. Now I suggest we sit down or I'm going to get a crook in my neck staring up at you."

He heard the smile in her voice and then saw it on her lips. It stirred to life something inside of him and for a moment he wondered if her smile was genuine or practiced and quickly came to the conclusion it was genuine. During his thirty-four years he had met women who'd been as phony as a four-dollar bill but he had a feeling Bella Bostwick wasn't one of them. In fact, she might be a little too real for her own good.

"I don't want that to happen," he said, easing down on her sofa and stretching his long legs out in front of him. He watched as she then eased down in the comfortable looking recliner he had bought Herman five years ago for his seventy-fifth birthday.

Jason figured this was probably one of the craziest things he'd ever done, sit with a woman in her living room in the middle of the day and converse with her while sipping tea. But he was doing it and at that moment, he couldn't imagine any other place he'd rather be.

Bella took a sip of her tea and studied Jason over the rim of her cup. Who was he? Why was she so attracted to him? And why was he attracted to her? And she knew the latter was true. She'd felt it that night at the ball and she could feel it now. He was able to bring out desires in her that she never felt before but for some reason she didn't feel threatened by those feelings. Instead, although she really didn't know him, she felt he was a powerhouse of strength, tenderness and protectiveness all rolled into one. She knew he would never hurt her.

"So, tell me about yourself Jason," she heard herself say, wanting so much to hear about the man who seemed to be taking up so much space in her living room as well as in her mind.

A smile touched his lips when he said, "I'm a West-moreland."

His words raised her curiosity up a notch. Was being a Westmoreland supposed to mean something? She hadn't heard any type of arrogance or egotism in his words, just a sense of pride, self-respect and honor.

"And what does being a Westmoreland mean?" she asked as she tucked her legs beneath her to get more comfortable in the chair.

She watched him take a sip of his tea. "There's a bunch of us, fifteen in fact," Jason said.

She nodded, taking in his response. "Fifteen?"

"Yes. And that's not counting the three Westmoreland wives and a cousin-in-law from Australia. In our family tree we've now become known as the Denver Westmorelands."

"Denver Westmorelands? Does that mean there are more Westmorelands in other parts of the country?"

"Yes, there are some who sprung from the Atlanta area. We have fifteen cousins there, as well. Most of them were at the Westmoreland charity ball."

An amused smile touched her lips. She recalled seeing them and remembered thinking how much they'd resembled in looks or height. Jason had been the only one she'd gotten a real good close-up view of, and the only one she'd held a conversation with before her uncle had practically dragged her away from the party that night.

She then decided to bring up something she'd detected at the ball. "You and my uncle Kenneth don't get along."

If her statement surprised him the astonishment was not reflected in his face. "No, we've never gotten along," he said as if the thought didn't bother him, in fact he preferred it that way.

She paused and waited on him to elaborate but he didn't. He just took another sip of tea.

"And why is that?"

He shrugged massive shoulders and the gesture made her body even more responsive to his. "I can't rightly say why we've never seen eye-to-eye on a number of things."

"What about my grandfather? Did you get along with him?"

He chuckled. "Actually I did. Herman and I had a good relationship that started back when I was kid. He taught me a lot about ranching and I enjoyed our chats."

She took a sip of her tea. "Did he ever mention anything about having a granddaughter?"

"No, but then I didn't know he had a son, either. The only family I knew about was Kenneth and their relationship was rather strained."

She nodded. She'd heard the story of how her father had left for college at the age of seventeen, never to return. Her uncle Kenneth claimed he wasn't sure what the disagreement had been between the two men since he himself had been a young kid at the time. David Bostwick had made his riches on the east coast, first as a land developer and then as an investor in all sorts of moneymaking ventures. That was how he'd met her mother, a Savannah socialite, daughter of a shipping magnate and ten years her senior. The marriage had been based more on increasing their wealth instead of love. She was well aware of both of her parents' supposedly discreet affairs.

And as far as Kenneth Bostwick was concerned, she knew that Herman's widowed father at the age of seventy married a thirty-something-year-old woman and Kenneth had been their only child. Bella gathered from bits and pieces she'd overheard from Kenneth's daughter, Elyse, that Kenneth and Herman had never gotten along because Herman thought Kenneth's mother, Belinda, hadn't been anything but a gold digger who married a man old enough to be her grandfather.

"Finding out Herman had a granddaughter came as a surprise to everyone around these parts."

Bella chuckled softly. "Yes, and it came as quite a surprise to me to discover I had a grandfather."

She saw the surprise that touched his face. "You didn't know about Herman?"

"No. I thought both my father's parents were dead. My father was close to forty when he married my mother and when I was in my teens he was in his fifties already so I assumed his parents were deceased since he never mentioned them. I didn't know about Herman until I got a summons to be present at the reading of the will. My parents didn't even mention anything about the funeral. They attended the services but only said they were leaving town to take care of business. I assumed it was one of their usual business trips. It was only when they returned that they mentioned that Herman's attorney had advised them that I was needed for the reading of the will in a week."

She pulled in a deep breath. "Needless to say, I wasn't happy that my parents had kept such a thing from me all those years. I felt whatever feud was between my father and grandfather was between them and should not have included me. I feel such a sense of loss at not having known Herman Bostwick."

Jason nodded. "He could be quite a character at times, trust me."

For some reason she felt she could trust him…and in fact, that she already did. "Tell me about him. I want to get to know the grandfather I never knew."

He smiled. "There's no way I can tell you everything about him in one day."

She returned the smile. "Then come back again for tea so we can talk. That is, if you don't mind."

She held her breath thinking he probably had a lot more things to do with his time than to sip tea with her. A man like him probably had other things on his mind when he was with someone of the opposite sex.

"No, I don't mind. In fact I'd rather enjoy it."

She inwardly sighed, suddenly feeling giddy, pleased. Jason Westmoreland was the type of man who could make his way into any woman's hot and wild fantasies, and he'd just agreed to indulge her by sharing tea with her occasionally to talk about the grandfather she'd never known.

"Well, I guess I'd better get back to work."

"And what do you do for a living?" she asked, without thinking about it.

"Several of my cousins and I are partners in a horse breeding and horse training venture. The horse that came in second last year at the Preakness was one of ours."

"Congratulations!"

"Thanks."

She then watched as he eased his body off her sofa to stand. And when he handed the empty teacup back to her, she felt her body tingle with the exchange when their hands touched and knew he'd felt it, as well.

"Thanks for the tea, Bella."

"You're welcome and you have an open invitation to come back for more."

He met her gaze, held it for a moment. "And I will."

Two

On Tuesday of the following week, Bella was in her car headed to town to purchase new appliances for her kitchen. Buying a stove and refrigerator might not be a big deal to some, but for her it would be a first. She was looking forward to it. Besides, it would get her mind off the phone call she'd gotten from her attorney first thing this morning.

Not wanting to think about the phone call, she thought about her friends back home instead. They had teased her that although she would be living out in the boondocks on a ranch, downtown Denver was half an hour away and that's probably where she would spend most of her time—shopping and attending various plays and parties. But she had discovered she liked being away from city life and hadn't missed it at all. She'd grown up in Savannah right on the ocean. Her parents' estate had been minutes from downtown and was the place where lavish parties were always held.

She had talked to her parents earlier today and found the conversation totally draining. Her father insisted she put the ranch up for sale and come home immediately. When the conversation ended she had been more determined than ever to keep as much distance between her and Savannah as possible.

She had been on the ranch for only three weeks and already the taste of freedom, to do whatever she wanted whenever she wanted, was a luxurious right she refused to give up. Although she missed waking up every morning to the scent of the ocean, she was becoming used to the crisp mountain air drenched in the rich fragrance of dahlias.

Her thoughts then shifted to something else or more precisely, someone else. Jason Westmoreland. Good to his word he had stopped by a few days ago to join her for tea. They'd had a pleasant conversation, and he'd told her more about her grandfather. She could tell Jason and Herman's relationship had been close. Part of her was glad that Jason had probably helped relieve Herman's loneliness.

Although her father refused to tell her what had happened to drive him away from home, she hoped to find out on her own. Her grandfather had kept a number of journals and she intended to start reading them this week. The only thing she knew from what Kenneth Bostwick had told her was that Herman's father, William, had remarried when Herman was in his twenties and married with a son of his own. That woman had been Kenneth's mother, which was why he was a lot younger than her father. In fact her father and Kenneth had few memories of each other since David Bostwick had left home for college at the age of seventeen.

Jason had also answered questions about ranching and assured her that the man she'd kept on as foreman had worked for her grandfather for a number of years and knew what he was doing. Jason hadn't stayed long but she'd enjoyed his visit.

She found Jason to be kind and soft-spoken and whenever he talked in that reassuring tone she would feel safe, protected and confident that no matter what decisions she made regarding her life and the ranch, it would be okay. He also gave her the impression that she could and would make mistakes and that would be okay, too, as long as she learned from those mistakes and didn't repeat them.

She had gotten to meet some of his family members, namely the women, when they'd all shown up a couple of days ago with housewarming goodies to welcome her to the community. Pamela, Chloe and Lucia had married into the family, and Megan and Bailey were Westmorelands by birth. They told her about Gemma, who was Megan and Bailey's sister and how she had gotten married earlier that year, moved with her husband to Australia and was expecting their first child.

Pamela and Chloe had brought their babies and being in their presence only reinforced a desire Bella always had of being a mother. She loved children and hoped to marry and have a houseful one day. And when she did, she intended for her relationship with them to be different than the one she had with her own parents.

The women had invited her to dinner at Pamela's home Friday evening so that she could meet the rest of the family. She thought the invitation to dinner was a nice gesture and downright neighborly on their part.

They were surprised she had already met Jason because he hadn't mentioned anything to them about meeting her.

She wasn't sure why he hadn't when all the evidence led her to believe the Westmorelands were a close-knit group. But then she figured men tended to keep their activities private and not share them with anyone. He said he would be dropping by for tea again tomorrow and she looked forward to his visit.

It was obvious there was still an intense attraction between them, yet he always acted honorably in her presence. He would sit across from her with his long legs stretched out in front of him and sip tea while she talked. She tried not to dominate the conversation but found he was someone she could talk to and someone who listened to what she had to say. She could see him now sitting there absorbed in whatever she said while displaying a ruggedness she found totally sexy.

And he had shared some things about himself. She knew he was thirty-four and a graduate of the University of Denver. He also shared with her how his parents and uncle and aunt had been killed in a plane crash when he was eighteen, leaving him and his fourteen siblings and cousins without parents. With admiration laced in his voice he had talked about his older brother Dillon and his cousin Ramsey and how the two men had been determined to keep the family together and how they had.

She couldn't help but compare his large family to her smaller one. Although she loved her parents she couldn't recall a time she and her parents had ever been close. While growing up they had relinquished her care to sitters while they jet-setted all over the country. At times she thought they'd forgotten she existed. When she got older she understood her father's obsession with trying to keep up with his young wife. Eventually she saw that obsession diminish when he found other interests and her mother did, as well.

That was why at times the idea of having a baby without a husband appealed to her, although doing such a thing would send her parents into cardiac arrest. But she couldn't concern herself with how her parents would react if she chose to go that route. Moving here was her first stab at emancipation and whatever she decided to do would be her decision. But for a woman who'd never slept with a man to contemplate having a baby from one was a bit much for her to absorb right now.

She pulled into the parking lot of one of the major appliance stores. When she returned home she would meet with her foreman to see how things were going. Jason had said such meetings were necessary and she should be kept updated on what went on at her ranch.

Moments later as she got out of her car she decided another thing she needed to do was buy a truck. *A truck*. She chuckled, thinking her mother would probably gag at the thought of her driving a truck instead of being chauffeured around in a car. But her parents had to realize and accept her life was changing and the luxurious life she used to have was now gone.

As soon as she entered the store a salesperson was right on her heels and it didn't take long to make the purchases she needed because she knew just what she wanted. She'd always thought stainless steel had a way of enhancing the look of a kitchen and figured sometime next year she would give the kitchen a total makeover with granite countertops and new tile flooring, as well. But she would take things one step at a time.

"Bella?"

She didn't have to turn to know who'd said her name. As far as she was concerned, no one could pronounce it in the same rugged yet sexy tone as Jason. Although she had just seen him a few days ago when he'd joined her for tea, there was something about seeing him now that sent sensations coursing through her.

She turned around and there he stood dressed in a pair of jeans that hugged his sinewy thighs and long, muscular legs, a blue chambray shirt and a lightweight leather jacket that emphasized the broadness of his shoulders.

She smiled up at him. "Jason, what a pleasant surprise."

It was a pleasant surprise for Jason, as well. He had walked into the store and immediately, like radar, he had picked up on her presence and all it took was following her scent to find her.

"Same here. I had to come into town to pick up a new hot water heater for the bunkhouse," he said, smiling down at her. He shoved his hands into his pockets; otherwise, he would have been tempted to pull her to him and kiss her. Kissing Bella was something he wanted but hadn't gotten around to doing. He didn't want to rush things and didn't want her to think his interest in her had anything to do with wanting to buy Hercules, because that wasn't the case. His interest in her was definitely one of want and need.

"I met the ladies in your family the other day. They came to pay me a visit," she said.

"Did they?"

"Yes."

He'd known they would eventually get around to

doing so. The ladies had discussed a visit to welcome her to the community.

"They're all so nice," she said

"I think they are nice, too. Did you get whatever you needed?" He wondered if she would join him for lunch if he were to ask.

"Yes, my refrigerator and stove will be delivered by the end of the week. I'm so excited."

He couldn't help but laugh. She was genuinely excited. If she got that excited over appliances he could imagine how she would react over jewelry. "Will you be in town for a while, Bella?"

"Yes. I have a meeting with Marvin later this evening."

He raised a brow. "Is everything all right?"

She nodded, smiling. "Yes. I'm just having a weekly meeting like you suggested."

He was glad she had taken his advice. "How about joining me for lunch? There's a place not far from here that serves several nice dishes."

She smiled up at him. "I'd love that."

Jason knew he would love it just as much. He had been thinking about her a lot, especially at night when he'd found it hard to sleep. She was getting to him. No, she had gotten to him. He didn't know of any other woman that he'd been this attracted to. There was something about her. Something that was drawing him to her on a personal level that he could not control. But then a part of him didn't want to control it. Nor did he want to fight it. He wanted to see how far it would go and where it would stop

"Do you want me to follow you there, Jason?"

No, he wanted her in the same vehicle with him. "We

can ride in my truck. Your car will be fine parked here until we return."

"Okay."

As he escorted her toward the exit, she glanced up at him. "What about your hot water heater?"

"I haven't picked it out yet but that's fine since I know the brand I want."

"All right."

Together they walked out of the store toward his truck. It was a beautiful day in May but when he felt her shiver beside him, he figured a beautiful day in Savannah would be a day in the eighties. Here in Denver if they got sixty-something degree weather in June they would be ecstatic.

He took his jacket off and placed it around her shoulders. She glanced up at him. "You didn't have to do that."

He smiled. "Yes, I did. I don't want you to get cold on me." She was wearing a pair of black slacks and a light blue cardigan sweater. As always she looked ultrafeminine.

And now she was wearing his jacket. They continued walking and when they reached his truck she glanced up and her gaze connected with his and he could feel electricity sparking to life between them. She looked away quickly, as if she'd been embarrassed that their attraction to each other was so obvious.

"Do you want your jacket back now?" she asked softly.

"No, keep it on. I like seeing you in it."

She blushed again and at that moment he got the most ridiculous notion that perhaps this sort of intense attraction between two people was sort of new to Bella. He wouldn't be surprised to discover that she had several innocent bones in her body; enough to shove him in another direction rather quickly. But for some reason he was staying put.

She nibbled on her bottom lip. "Why do you like seeing me in it?"

"Because I do. And because it's mine and you're in it."

He wasn't sure if what he'd said made much sense or if she was confused even more. But what he *was* sure about was that he was determined to find out just how much Bella Bostwick knew about men. And what she didn't know he was going to make it his business to teach her.

Bella was convinced there was nothing more compelling than the feel of wearing the jacket belonging to a man whose very existence represented true masculinity. It permeated her with his warmth, his scent and his aura in every way. She was filled with an urge to get more, to know more and to feel more of Jason Westmoreland. And as she stared at him through the car's window as he pulled out his cell phone to make arrangements for their lunch, she couldn't help but feel the hot rush of blood in her veins while heat churned deep down inside of her.

And there lay the crux of her problem. As beguiling as the feelings taking over her senses, making ingrained curiosity get the best of her, she knew better than to step beyond the range of her experience. That range didn't extend beyond what the nuns at the private Catholic schools she'd attended most of her life had warned her about. It was a range good girls just didn't go beyond.

Jason was the type of man women dreamed about. He was what fantasies were made of. She watched him ease his phone back into the pocket of his jeans, walk around the front of his truck to get in. He was the type of man a woman would love to snuggle up with on a cold Colorado winter night...especially the kind her parents and uncle had said she would have to endure. Just the thought of being with him in front of a roaring fire that blazed in a fireplace would be an unadulterated fantasy come true for any woman.... And her greatest fear.

"You're comfortable?" he asked, placing a wide-brimmed Stetson on his head.

She glanced over at him and she held his gaze for a moment and then nodded. "Yes, I'm fine. Thanks."

"You're welcome."

He backed up the truck and then they headed out of the parking lot in silence but she was fully aware of his hands that gripped the steering wheel. They were large and strong hands and she could imagine those same hands gripping her. That thought made heat seep into every cell and pore of her body, percolating her bones and making her surrender to something she'd never had before.

Her virginal state had never bothered her before and it didn't really bother her now except the unknown was making the naughtiness in her come out. It was making her anticipate things she was better off not getting.

"You've gotten quiet on me, Bella," Jason said.

She glanced over at him and again met his gaze thinking, yes she had. But she figured he didn't want to hear her thoughts out loud and certain things she needed to keep to herself.

"Sorry," she said. "I was thinking about Friday," she decided to say.

"Friday?"

"Yes. Pamela invited me to dinner."

"She did?"

Bella heard the surprise in his voice. "Yes. She said it would be the perfect opportunity to meet everyone. It seems all of my neighbors are Westmorelands. You're just the one living the closest to me."

"And what makes you so preoccupied about Friday?"

"Meeting so many of your family members."

He chuckled. "You'll survive."

"Thanks for the vote of confidence." Then she said, "Tell me about them." He had already told her some but she wanted to hear more. And the ladies who came to visit had also shared some of their family history with her. But she wanted to hear his version just to hear the husky sound of his voice, to feel how it would stir across her skin and tantalize several parts of her body.

"You already met the ones who think they run things, namely the women."

She laughed. "They don't?"

"We let them think that way because we're slowly getting outnumbered. Although Gemma is in Australia she still has a lot to say and whenever we take a vote about anything, of course she sides with the women."

She grinned. "You all actually take votes on stuff?"

"Yes, we believe in democracy. The last time we voted we had to decide where Christmas dinner would be held. Usually we hold everything at Dillon's because he has the main family house, but his kitchen was being renovated so we voted to go to Ramsey's."

"All of you have homes?"

"Yes. When we each turned twenty-five we inherited one hundred acres. It was fun naming my own spread."

"Yours is Jason's Place, right?"

He smiled over at her. "That's right."

While he'd been talking her body had responded to the sound of his voice as if it was on a mission to capture each and every nuance. She inhaled deeply and they began chatting again but this time about her family. He'd been honest about his family so she decided to be honest about hers.

"My parents and I aren't all that close and I can't remember a time that we were. They didn't support my move out here," she said and wondered why she'd wanted to share that little detail.

"Is it true that Kenneth is upset you didn't sell the land to Myers Smith?" he asked.

She nodded slowly. "Yes, he told me himself that he thinks I made a mistake in deciding to move here and is looking forward to the day I fail so he can say, 'I told you so.'"

Jason shook his head, finding it hard to believe this was a family member who was hoping for her failure. "Are he and your father close?"

Bella chuckled softly. "They barely know each other. According to Dad he was already in high school when Kenneth was born, although technically Kenneth is my father's half uncle. My father's grandfather married Kenneth's mother who was twenty-five years his junior."

"Do you have any other family, like cousins?"

She shook her head. "Both my parents were the only children. Of course Uncle Kenneth has a son and daughter but they hadn't spoken to me since the reading of the will. Uncle Kenneth only spoke to me when he thought I'd be selling the ranch and livestock to his friend."

By the time he had brought the truck to a stop in front of a huge building, she had to wipe tears of laughter from her eyes when he'd told her about all the trouble the younger Westmorelands had gotten into.

"I just can't imagine your cousin Bailey—who has such an innocent look about her—being such a hellraiser while growing up."

Jason laughed. "Hey, don't let the innocent act fool you. The cousins Aiden and Adrian are at Harvard and Bane joined the navy. We talked Bailey into hanging around here to attend college so we could keep an eye on her."

He chuckled and then added, "It turned out to be a mistake when she began keeping an eye on us instead."

When he turned off the truck's engine she glanced through the windshield at the building looming in front of them and raised a brow. "This isn't a restaurant?"

He glanced over at her. "No, it's not. It's the Blue Ridge Management, a company my father and uncle founded over forty years ago. After they were killed Dillon and Ramsey took over. Ramsey eventually left Dillon in charge to become a sheep rancher and Dillon is currently CEO."

He glanced out the windshield to look up at the forty-story building with a pensive look on his face and moments later added, "My brother Riley holds an upper management position here. My cousins Zane and Derringer, as well as myself, worked for the company after college until last year when we decided to join the Montana Westmorelands in the horse training and breeding business."

He smiled. "I guess you can say that nine-to-five gig was never our forte. Like Ramsey we prefer being outdoors."

She nodded and followed his gaze to the building. "And we're eating lunch here?"

He glanced over at her. "Yes, I have my office that I still use from time to time to conduct business. I called ahead and Dillon's secretary took care of everything for me."

A few moments later they were walking into the massive lobby of Blue Ridge Land Management and the first thing Bella noticed was the huge, beautifully decorated atrium with a waterfall amidst a replica of mountains complete with blooming flowers and other types of foliage. After stopping at the security guard station they caught an elevator up to the executive floor.

"I remember coming up here a lot with my dad," Jason said softly, reflecting on that time. "Whenever he would work on the weekends, he would gather us all together to get us out of Mom's hair for a while. Once we got up to the fortieth floor we knew he would probably find something for us to do."

He chuckled and then added, "But just in case he didn't. I would always travel with a pack of crayons in my back pocket."

Bella smiled. She could just imagine Jason and his six brothers crowded on the elevator with their father. Although he would be working they would have gotten to spend the day with him nonetheless. She couldn't ever recall a time her father had taken her to work with him. In fact she hadn't known where the Bostwick Firm had been located until she was well into her teens. Her mother never worked outside the home but was mainly the hostess for the numerous parties her parents would give.

It seemed the ride to the top floor took forever. A few

times the elevator stopped to let people either on or off. Some of them recognized Jason and he took the time to inquire about the family members he knew, especially their children or grandchildren.

The moment they stepped off the elevator onto the fortieth floor Bella could tell immediately that this was where all the executive offices were located. The furniture was plush and the carpeting thick and luxurious looking. She was quickly drawn to huge paintings of couples adorning the walls in the center of the lobby. Intrigued she moved toward them.

"These are my parents," Jason said, coming to stand by her side. "And the couple in the picture over there is my aunt and uncle. My father and Uncle Thomas were close, barely fourteen months apart in age. And my mother and Aunt Susan got along beautifully and were just as close as sisters."

"And they died together," she whispered softly. It was a statement not a question since he had already told her what had happened when they'd all died in a plane crash. Bella studied the portrait of his parents in detail. Jason favored his father a lot but he definitely had his mother's mouth.

"She was beautiful," she said. "So was your aunt Susan. I take it Ramsey and Chloe's daughter was named after her?"

Jason nodded. "Yes, and she's going to grow up to be a beauty just like her grandmother."

She glanced over at him. "And what was your mother's name?"

"Clarisse. And my father was Adam." Jason then looked down at his watch. "Come on. Our lunch should have arrived by now."

He surprised her when he took her arm and led her

toward a bank of offices and stopped at one in particular with his name on it. She felt her heart racing. Although he hadn't called it as such, she considered this lunch a date.

That thought was reinforced when he opened the door to his office and she saw the table set for lunch. The room was spacious and had a downtown view of Denver. The table, completely set with everything, including a bottle of wine, had been placed by the window so they could enjoy the view while they ate.

"Jason, the table and the view are beautiful. Thanks for inviting me to lunch."

"You're welcome," he said, pulling a chair out for her. "There's a huge restaurant downstairs for the employees but I thought we'd eat in here for privacy."

"That's considerate of you."

And done for purely selfish reasons, Jason thought as he took the chair across from her. He liked having her all to himself. Although he wasn't a tea drinker, he had become one and looked forward to visiting her each week to sit down and converse while drinking tea. He enjoyed her company. He glanced over at her and their gazes connected. Their response to each other always amazed him because it seemed so natural and out of control. He couldn't stop the heat flowing all through his body at that precise moment even if he wanted to.

He doubted she knew she had a dazed look in the depths of her dark eyes or that today everything about her looked soft, feminine but not overly so. Just to the right degree to make a man appreciate being a man.

She slowly broke eye contact with him to lift the lid off the platter and when she glanced back up she was smiling brightly. "Spaghetti."

He couldn't help but return her smile. "Yes. I recall

you saying the other day how much you enjoyed Italian food." In fact they had talked about a number of things in the hour he had been there.

"I do love Italian food," she said excitedly, taking a hold of her fork.

He poured wine into their glasses and glanced over and caught her slurping up a single strand of spaghetti through a pair of luscious lips. His gut clenched and when she licked her lips he couldn't help but envy the noodle.

When she caught him staring she blushed, embarrassed at being caught doing something so inelegant. "Sorry. I know that showed bad manners but I couldn't resist." She smiled. "It was the one thing I always wanted to do around my parents whenever we ate spaghetti that I couldn't do."

He chuckled. "No harm done. In fact you can slurp the rest of it if you'd like. It's just you and me."

She grinned. "Thanks, but I better not." He then watched as she took her fork in her hand, preparing to eat the rest of her spaghetti in the classical and cultured way.

"I take it your parents were strong disciplinarians," he said, taking a sip of his wine.

Her smile slowly faded. "They still are or at least they try to be. Even now they will stop at nothing to get me back to Savannah so they can keep an eye on me. I got a call from my attorney this morning warning me they've possibly found a loophole in the trust fund my grandparents established for me before they died."

He lifted a brow. "What kind of a loophole?"

"One that says I'm supposed to be married after the first year. If that's true I have less than three months," she said in disgust. "I'm sure they're counting on me returning to Savannah to marry Hugh."

He sipped his wine. "Hugh?"

She met his gaze and he could see the troubled look in hers. "Yes, Hugh Pierce. His family comes from Savannah's old money and my parents have made up their minds that Hugh and I are a perfect match."

He watched her shoulders rise and fall after releasing several sighs. Evidently the thought of becoming Mrs. Hugh Pierce bothered her. Hell, the thought bothered him, as well.

In a way he should be overjoyed, elated, that there was a possibility she was moving back to Savannah. That meant her ranch and Hercules would probably be up for sale. And when they were, he would be ready to make her an offer he hoped she wouldn't refuse. He knew he wasn't the only one wanting the land and no telling how many others wanted Hercules, but he was determined that the prized stallion wouldn't fall into anyone's hands but his.

And yet, he wasn't overjoyed or elated at the thought that she would return to Savannah.

He got the impression her parents were controlling people or at least they tried to be. He began eating, wondering why her parents wanted to shove this Hugh Pierce down her throat when she evidently wasn't feeling the guy. Would they coerce her to marry someone just because the man came from "old money"?

He forced the thought to the back of his mind, thinking who she ended up marrying was no concern of his. But making sure his name headed the list as a potential buyer for her ranch and livestock was. He glanced over at her. "When will you know what you'll have to do?"

She looked up after taking a sip of her wine. "I'm not sure. I have a good attorney but I have to admit my parents' attorney is more experienced in such matters. In other words, he's crafty as sin. I'm sure when my grandparents drew up my trust they thought they were looking out for my future because in their social circles, ideally, a young woman married by her twenty-sixth birthday. For her to attend college was just a formality since she was expected to marry a man who had the means to take care of her."

"And your parents have no qualms in forcing you to marry?"

"No, not one iota," she said without pause. "They don't truly care about my happiness. All they care about is that they would be proving once again they control my life and always will."

He heard the trembling in her voice and when she looked down as to study her silverware, he knew her composure was being threatened. At that moment, something inside of him wanted to get up, pull her into his arms and tell her things would be all right. But he couldn't rightly say that. He had no way of knowing they would be for her, given the situation she was in. Actually it was her problem not his. Still another part of him couldn't help regretting that her misfortune could end up being his golden opportunity.

"I thought I'd finally gotten free of my parents' watchful eyes at college, only to discover they had certain people in place, school officials and professors, keeping tabs on me and reporting to them on my behavior," she said, interrupting his thoughts.

"And I thought, I truly believed, the money I'm getting from my trust fund and inheriting the ranch were my way of living my life the way I want and an end to being under my parents' control. I was going to exert my freedom for the first time in my life."

She paused briefly. "Jason. I really love it here. I've been able to live the way I want, do the things I want. It's a freedom I've never had and I don't want to give it up."

They sat staring at each other for what seemed like several mind-numbing moments and then Jason spoke. "Then don't give it up. Fight them for what you want."

Her shoulders slumped again. "Although I plan to try, it's easier said than done. My father is a well-known and powerful man in Savannah and a lot of the judges are his personal friends. For anyone to even try something as archaic as forcing someone to marry is ludicrous. But my parents will do it with their friends' help if it brings me to heel."

Once again Bella fell silent for a moment. "When I received word about Herman and confronted my father as to why he never told me about his life here in Denver, he wouldn't tell me, but I've been reading my grandfather's journals. He claims my father hated living here while growing up. His mother had visited this area from Savannah, met Herman and fell in love and never went back east. Her family disowned her for it. But after college my father moved to Savannah and sought out his maternal grandparents and they were willing to accept him in their good graces but only if he never reminded them of what they saw as their daughter's betrayal, so he didn't."

She then straightened her shoulders and forced a smile to her lips. "Let's change the subject," she suggested. "Thinking about my woes is rather depressing and you've made lunch too nice for me to be depressed about anything."

They enjoyed the rest of their meal conversing about other things. He told her about his horse breeding business and about how he and the Atlanta Westmorelands had discovered they were related through his great-grandfather Raphel Westmoreland.

"Was your grandfather really married to all those women?" she asked after he told her the tale of how Raphel had become a black sheep in the family after running off in the early nineteen hundreds with the preacher's wife and all the other wives he supposedly collected along the way.

He took another sip of wine. "That's what everyone is trying to find out. We need to know if there are any more Westmorelands out there. Megan is hiring a private detective to help solve the puzzle about Raphel's wives. We've eliminated two and now we have two more to check out."

When they finished the main course Jason used his cell phone to call downstairs to say they were ready for dessert. Moments later banana pudding was delivered to them. Bella thought the dessert was simply delicious. She usually didn't eat a lot of sweets but once she'd taken a bite she couldn't help but finish the whole thing.

A short while later, after they'd devoured the dessert with coffee, Jason checked his watch. "We're right on schedule. I'll take you back in time to get your car so you can make your meeting with Marvin."

Jason stood, rounded the table and reached for her hand. The instant they touched it seemed a rush of heated sensations tore through the both of them at the same time. It was absorbed in their bones, tangled their flesh and he all but shuddered under the impact. The alluring scent of her filled his nostrils and his breath was freed on a ragged sigh.

Some part of his brain told him to take a step back and put distance between them. But then another part told him he was facing the inevitable. There had been this blazing attraction, this tantalizing degree of lust between them from the beginning. For him it had been since the moment he had seen her when she'd entered the ballroom with Kenneth Bostwick. He had known then he wanted her.

They stared at each other and for a second he thought she would avert her gaze from his but she didn't. She couldn't resist him any more than he could resist her and they both knew it, which was probably why, when he took a step closer and began lowering his head, she went on tiptoes and lifted her mouth to meet his.

The moment their lips connected, a low, guttural sound rumbled from deep in his throat and he deepened the kiss the moment she wrapped her arms around his neck. His tongue slid easily into her mouth, exploring one side and then another, as well as all the areas in between before tangling with her own, mating deeply, and when she reciprocated the move sent a jolt of desire all through his bones.

And then it was on.

Holy crap. Hunger the likes he'd never felt before infiltrated his mind. He felt a sexual connection with her that he'd never felt with any woman before. As his tongue continued to slide against hers, parts of him felt primed and ready to explode at any moment. Never had he encountered such overwhelming passion, such blatant desire and raw primal need.

His mouth was doing a good job tasting her, but the rest of him wanted to feel her, draw her closer into his arms. On instinct he felt her lean into him, plastering their bodies from breast to knee and as Jason deepened the kiss even more, he groaned, wondering if he would never get enough of her.

Bella was feeling the same way about Jason. No man had ever held her this close, taken her mouth this passionately and made sensations she'd never felt before rush through her quicker than the speed of light.

And she felt him, his erection, rigid and throbbing, against her middle, pressing hard at the juncture of her thighs, making her feel sensations there—right there—she hadn't felt before. It was doing more than just tingling. She was left aching in that very spot. She felt like a mass of kerosene and he was a torch set to ignite her, making her explode into flames. He was all solid muscle pressing against her and she wanted it all. She wanted him. She wasn't sure what wanting him entailed but she knew he was the only man who made her feel this way. He was the only man she wanted to make her feel this way.

When at last he drew his mouth away from her, his face remained close. Acting by instinct, she took her tongue and licked around his lips from corner to corner, not ready to relinquish the taste of him. When a guttural sound emitted from his throat, need rammed through her and when she tilted her lips toward his, he took her mouth once again. He eased his tongue into her mouth like it had every right to be there and at the moment she was of the conclusion that it did.

He slowly broke off the kiss and stared into her face for a long moment before caressing his thumb across her lips then running his fingers through the curls on her head.

"I guess we better leave now so you won't miss your meeting," he said in a deep, husky tone.

Unable to utter a single word she merely nodded.

And when he took her hand and entwined her fingers in his, the sensations she'd felt earlier were still strong, nearly overpowering, but she was determined to fight it this time. And every time after that. She could not become involved with anyone, especially someone like Jason. And especially not now.

She had enough on her plate in dealing with the ranch and her parents. She had to keep her head on straight and not get caught up in the desires of the flesh. She didn't need a lover; she needed a game plan.

And as Jason led her out of his office, she tried sorting out all the emotions she was feeling. She'd just been kissed senseless and now she was trying to convince herself that no matter what, it couldn't happen again.

Only problem with that was her mind was declaring one thing and her body was claiming another.

Three

He was in serious trouble.

Jason rubbed his hand across his face as he watched Bella rush off toward her car. He made sure she had gotten inside and driven off before pulling out of the parking lot behind her. The Westmoreland men were known to have high testosterone levels but his had never given him pause until today and only with Bella Bostwick.

He wouldn't waste his time wondering why he had kissed her since he knew the reason. She was walking femininity at its finest, temptation not too many men could resist and a lustful shot in any man's arms. He had gotten a sampling of all three. And it hadn't been a little taste but a whole whopping one. Now that he knew her flavor he wanted to savor it again and again and again.

When he brought his truck to a stop at a traffic light

he checked his watch. Bella wasn't the only one who had a meeting this afternoon. He, Zane and Derringer had a conference call with their partners in Montana in less than an hour. He hadn't forgotten about the meeting but spending time with Bella had been something he hadn't been willing to shorten. Now with the taste of her still lingering in his mouth, he was glad he hadn't.

He shook his head, still finding it hard to believe just how well they had connected with that kiss, which made him wonder how they would connect in other ways and places...like in the bedroom.

The thought of her naked, thighs opened while he entered her was something he couldn't get out of his mind. He was burning for her and although he'd like to think it was only a physical attraction he wasn't sure that was the case. But then if it wasn't the case, what was it?

He didn't get a chance to think any further because at that moment his cell phone rang. He pulled it off his belt and saw it was his cousin Derringer. The newlywed of just a little over a month had been the last person he'd thought would fall in love with any woman. But he had and Jason could see why. Lucia was as precious as they came and everyone thought she was a great addition to the Westmoreland family.

"Yes, Derringer?"

"Hey, man, where are you? Did you forget about today's meeting?"

Jason couldn't help but smile as he remembered how he'd called to ask Derringer the same question since he'd gotten married. It seemed these days it was hard for his cousin to tear himself away from his wife at times.

"No, I didn't forget and I'm less than thirty minutes away."

"Okay. And I hear your lady is joining the family for dinner on Friday night."

He considered that for a moment. Had anyone else made that comment he probably would have gotten irritated by it, but Derringer was Derringer and the two people who knew more than anyone that he didn't have a "lady" were his cousins Derringer and Zane. Knowing that was the case he figured Derringer was fishing for information.

"I don't have a *lady* and you very well know it, Derringer."

"Do I? If that's the case when did you become a tea sipper?"

He laughed as his gaze held steady to the road. "Ah, I see our precious Bailey has been talking."

"Who else? Bella might have mentioned it to the ladies when they went visiting, but of course it's Bailey who's decided you have the hots for the Southern belle. And those were Bailey's words not mine."

"Thanks for clarifying that for me." The hots weren't all he had for Bella Bostwick. Blood was pumping fast and furious in his veins at the thought of the kiss they had shared.

"No problem. So level with me, Jason. What's going on with you and the Southern Bella?"

Jason smiled. The Southern Bella fit her. But then so did the Sensuous Bella. The Sexy Bella. The Sumptuous Bella. "And what makes you think something is going on?"

"I know you."

True. Derringer and Zane knew him better than any of the other Westmorelands because they'd always been close, thick as thieves while growing up. "I admit I'm attracted to her but what man wouldn't be? Otherwise, it's not that serious."

"You sure?"

Jason's hand tightened on his steering wheel—that was the crux of his problem. When it came to Bella the only thing he was sure about was that he wanted her in a way he'd never wanted any other woman. When they'd kissed she kissed him back in a way that had his body heating up just thinking how her tongue had mated with his. He had loved the way her silken curls had felt flowing through his fingers and how perfect their bodies fit together.

He was probably treading on dangerous ground but for reasons he didn't quite understand, he couldn't admit to being sure right now. So instead of outright lying he decided to plead the fifth by saying, "I'll get back to you on that."

Irritation spread all through his gut at the thought that he hadn't given Derringer an answer mainly because he couldn't. And for a man who'd always been decisive when it came to a woman's place in his heart, he could just imagine what Derringer was thinking.

He was trying not to think the same thing himself. Hell, he'd only set out to be a good neighbor and then realized how much he enjoyed her company. And then there had been the attraction he hadn't been able to overlook.

"I'll see you when you get here, Jason. Have a safe drive in," Derringer said without further comment about Bella.

"Will do."

Bella stood staring out her bedroom window at the mountains. Her meeting with Marvin had been informative as well as a little overwhelming. But she had been able to follow everything the man had said. Heading the list was Hercules. The horse was restless, agitated and it seemed when Hercules wasn't in a good mood everybody knew it.

According to Marvin, Hercules hadn't been ridden in a while mainly because very few men would go near him. The only man capable to handling Hercules was Jason. The same Jason she had decided to avoid from now on. She recognized danger when she saw it and in this case it was danger she could feel. Physically.

Even now she could remember Jason mesmerizing her with his smile, seducing her with his kiss and making her groan over and over again. And there was the way his gaze had scanned over her body while in the elevator as they left his office after lunch, or the hot, lusty look he gave her when she got out of the truck at the appliance store. That look had her rushing off as if a pack of pit bulls were nipping at her heels.

And last but not least were Jason's hands on her. Those big, strong hands had touched her in places that had made her pause for breath, had made sensations overtake her and had made her put her guard up in a way she didn't feel safe in letting down.

Of course she'd known they were attracted to each other from the first, but she hadn't expected that attraction to become so volatile and explosive. And she'd experienced all that from just one kiss. Heaven help them if they went beyond kissing.

If he continued to come around, if he continued to spend time with her in any way, they would be tempted to go beyond that. Today proved she was virtually putty in his hands and she didn't want to think about what that could mean if it continued. She liked it but then she was threatened by it. She was just getting to feel free and the last thing she wanted to be was held in bondage by anything, especially by emotions she couldn't quite understand. She wasn't ready to become the other part of anyone. Jeez, she was just finding herself, enjoying her newfound independence. She didn't want to give it up before experiencing it fully.

At that moment her cell phone went off and she rolled her eyes when she saw the caller was her mother. She pulled in a deep breath before saying, "Yes, Mother?"

"I'm sure you've heard from your attorney about that little stipulation we found out about in your trust fund. My mother was definitely smart to think of it."

Bella frowned. "Yes, I heard all about it." Of course Melissa Bostwick would take the time to call and gloat. And of course she wanted to make it seem that they had discovered the stipulation by accident when the truth was that they'd probably hired a team of attorneys to look for anything in the trust fund they could use against her to keep her in line. If they had their way she would be dependent on them for life.

"Good. Your father and I expect you to stop this nonsense immediately and come home."

"Sorry, Mom, but I am home."

"No, you're not and if you continue with this fool-ishness you will be sorry. With no money coming in, what on earth will you do?"

"Get a job I guess."

"Don't be ridiculous."

"I'm being serious. Sorry you can't tell the difference."

There was a pause and then her mother asked, "Why do you always want to have your way?"

"Because it's my way to have. I'm twenty-five for

heaven's sake. You and Dad need to let me live my own life."

"We will but not there, and Hugh's been asking about you."

"That's nice. Is there anything else you wanted, Mom?"

"For you to stop being difficult."

"If wanting to live my life the way I want is being difficult then get prepared for more difficult days ahead. Goodbye, Mom."

Out of respect Bella didn't hang up the phone until she heard her mother's click. And when she did she clicked off and shook her head. Her parents were so sure they had her where they wanted her.

And that possibility bothered her more than anything.

Jason glanced around the room. All of his male cousins had Bella to the side conversing away with her. No doubt they were as fascinated by her intellect as well as her beauty. And things had been that way since she'd arrived. More than once he'd sent Zane dirty looks that basically told his cousin to back off. Why he'd done such a thing he wasn't sure. He and Bella weren't an item or anything of the sort.

In fact, to his way of thinking, she was acting rather coolly toward him. Although she was polite enough, no one would have thought he had devoured her mouth the way he had three days ago in his office. And maybe that was the reason she was acting this way. No one was supposed to know. It was their secret. Right?

Wrong.

He knew his family well, a lot better than she did. Their acting like cordial acquaintances only made them suspect. His brother Riley had already voiced his suspicions. "Trouble in paradise with the Southern Bella?"

He'd frown and had been tempted to tell Riley there was no trouble in paradise because he and Bella didn't have that kind of relationship. They had kissed only once for heaven's sake. Twice, if you were to take into consideration that he'd kissed her a second time that day before leaving his office.

So, okay, they had kissed twice. No big deal. He drew in a deep breath wondering if it wasn't a big deal, why was he making it one? Why had he come early and anticipated her arrival like a kid waiting for Christmas to get here?

Everyone who knew him, especially his family, was well aware that he dated when it suited him and his reputation with women was nothing like Derringer's had been or Zane's was. It didn't come close. The thought of meeting someone and getting married and having a family was something at the bottom of his list, but at least he didn't mind claiming it was on his list. That was something some of his other single brothers and cousins refused to do.

"You're rather quiet tonight, Jason."

He glanced over and saw his cousin Bailey had come to stand beside him and knew why she was there. She wanted to not just pick his brain but to dissect his mind. "I'm no quieter than usual, Bail."

She tilted her head and looked up at him. "Hmm, I think you are. Does Bella have anything to do with it?"

He took a sip of his wine. "And what makes you think that?"

She shrugged. "Because you keep glancing over there at her when you think no one is looking."

"That's not true."

She smiled. "Yes, it is. You probably don't realize you're doing it."

He frowned. Was that true? Had he been that obvious whenever he'd glanced over at Bella? Of course someone like Bailey—who made it her business to keep up with everything and everyone or tried to—would notice such a thing.

"I thought we were just having dinner," he decided to say. "I didn't know it was an all-out dinner party."

Bailey grinned. "I remember the first time Ramsey brought Chloe to introduce her to the family. He'd thought the same thing."

Nodding, he remembered that time. "Only difference in that is that Ramsey *brought* Chloe. I didn't bring Bella nor did I invite her."

"Are you saying you wished she wasn't here?"

He hated when Bailey tried putting words into his mouth. And speaking of mouth…he glanced across the room to Bella and watched hers move and couldn't help remembering all he'd done to that mouth when he'd kissed her.

"Jason?"

He then recalled what Bailey had asked him and figured until he gave her an answer she wasn't going anywhere. "No, that's not what I'm saying and you darn well know it. I don't have a problem with Bella being here. I think it's important for her to get to know her neighbors."

But did his brothers and cousins have to stay in her face, hang on to her every word and check her out so thoroughly? He knew everyone who hadn't officially met her had been taken with her the moment Dillon had opened the door for her. She had walked in with a gracefulness and pristine elegance that made every male in the house appreciate not only her beauty but her poise, refinement and charming personality.

Her outfit, an electric-blue wrap dress with a flattering scoop neckline and a hem line that hit just above her knees greatly emphasized her small waist, firm breasts and shapely legs, and looked stylishly perfect on her. He would admit that his heart had slammed hard in his chest the moment she'd entered the room.

"Well, dinner is about to be served. You better hope you get a seat close to her. It won't take much for the others to boot you out the way." She then walked off.

He glanced back over to where Bella was standing and thought that no one would boot him out the way when it came to Bella. They better not even try.

Bella smiled at something Zane had said while trying not to glance across the room at Jason. He had spoken to her when she'd first arrived but since then had pretty much kept his distance, preferring to let his brothers and cousins keep her company.

You would never know they had been two people who'd almost demolished the mouths right off their faces a few days ago. But then maybe that was the point. Maybe he didn't want anyone to know. Come to think of it, she'd never asked if he even had a girlfriend. For all she knew he might have one. Just because he'd dropped by for tea didn't mean anything other than he was neighborly. And she had to remember that he had never gotten out of the way with her.

Until that day in his office.

What had made him want to kiss her? There had

been this intense chemistry between them from the first, but neither of them had acted on it until that day. Had stepping over those boundaries taken their relationship to a place where it couldn't recover? She truly hoped not. He was a nice person, a charmer if ever there was one. And although she'd decided that distance between them was probably for the best right now, she did want him to remain her friend.

"Pam's getting everyone's attention for dinner," Dillon said as he approached the group. "Let me escort you to the dining room," he offered and tucked Bella's arm beneath his.

She smiled at him. The one thing she noticed was that all the Westmoreland men resembled in some way. "Thank you."

She glanced over at Jason. Their gazes met and she felt it, the same sensations she felt whenever he was near her. That deep stirring in the pit of her stomach had her trying to catch her breath.

"You okay?" Dillon asked her.

She glanced up and saw concern in his deep dark eyes. He'd followed her gaze and noted it had lit on his brother. "Yes, I'm fine."

She just hoped what she'd said was true.

Jason wasn't surprised to discover he had been placed beside Bella at the dinner table. The women in the family tended to be matchmakers when they set their minds to it, which he could overlook considering three of them were all happily married themselves. The other two, Megan and Bailey, were in it for the ride.

He dipped his head, lower than he'd planned, to ask Bella if she was enjoying herself, and when she turned her head to look at him their lips nearly touched. He came close to ignoring everyone sitting at the table and giving in to the temptation to kiss her.

She must have read his mind and a light blush spread into her cheeks. He swallowed, pulled his lips back. "Are you having a good time?"

"Yes. And I appreciate your family for inviting me."

"And I'm sure they enjoy having you here," he said. Had she expected him to invite her? He shrugged off the thought as wrong. There had been no reason for him to invite her to meet his family. Come to think of it, he had never invited a woman home for dinner. Not even Emma Phillips and they'd dated close to a year before she tried giving him an ultimatum.

The meal went off without a hitch with various conversations swirling around the table. Megan informed everyone that the private investigator she had hired to dig deeper into their great-grandfather Raphel's past was Rico Claiborne, who just happened to be the brother of Jessica and Savannah who were married to their cousins Chase and Durango. Rico, whom Megan hadn't yet met, was flying into Denver at some point in time to go over the information he'd collected on what was supposed to be Raphel's third wife.

By the time dinner was over and conversations wound down it was close to ten o'clock. Someone suggested given the lateness of the hour that Bella be escorted back home. Several of his cousins spoke up to do the honor and Jason figured he needed to end the nonsense once and for all and said in a voice that brooked no argument, "I'll make sure Bella gets home."

He noticed that all conversation automatically ceased and no one questioned his announcement. "Ready to go?" he asked Bella softly.

"Yes."

She thanked everyone and openly gave his cousins and brothers hugs. It wasn't hard to tell that they all liked her and had enjoyed her visit. After telling everyone good-night he followed her out the door.

Bella glanced out her rearview mirror and saw Jason was following her at a safe distance. She laughed, thinking when it came to Jason there wasn't a safe zone. Just knowing he was anywhere within her area was enough to rattle her. Even sitting beside him at dinner had been a challenge for her, but thanks to the rest of his family who kept lively conversation going on, she was able to endure his presence and the sexual tension she'd felt. Each time he talked to her and she looked into his face and focused on his mouth, she would remember that same mouth mating with hers.

A sigh of relief escaped her lips when they pulled into her yard. Figuring it would be dark when she returned she had left lights burning outside and her yard was practically glowing. She parked her car and was opening the door to get out when she saw Jason already standing there beside it. Her breathing quickened and panic set in. "You don't need to walk me to the door, Jason," she said quickly.

"I want to," he said simply.

Annoyance flashed in her eyes when she recalled how he'd gone out of his way most of the evening to avoid her. "Why would you?"

He gave her a look. "Why wouldn't I?" Instead of waiting for her to respond he took her hand in his and headed toward her front door.

Fine! she thought, fuming inside and dismissing the temptation to pull her hand away from his. Because her foreman lived on the ranch, she knew the last thing she needed to do was make a scene with Jason outside under the bright lights. He stood back while she unlocked the door and she had a feeling he intended to make sure she was safely inside before leaving. She was right when he followed her inside.

When he closed the door behind them she placed her hands on her hips and opened her mouth to say what was on her mind, but he beat her to the punch. "Was I out of line when I kissed you that day, Bella?"

The softly spoken question gave her pause and she dropped her hands to her side. No, he hadn't been out of line mainly because she'd wanted the kiss. She had wanted to feel his mouth on hers, his tongue tangling with her own. And if she was downright truthful about it, she would admit to wanting his hands on her, all over her, touching her in ways no man had touched her before.

He was waiting for her response.

"No, you weren't out of line."

"Then why the coldness today?"

She tilted her chin. "I can be asking you the same thing, Jason. You weren't Mr. Congeniality yourself to-night."

He didn't say anything for a moment but she could tell her comment had hit a mark with him. "No, I wasn't," he admitted.

Although she had made the accusation she was stunned by the admission. It had caught her off guard. "Why?" She knew the reason for her distance but was curious to know the reason for his.

"Ladies first."

"Fine," she said, placing her purse on the table. "We

might as well get this little talk over with. Would you like something to drink?"

"Yes," he said, rubbing his hand down his face in frustration. "A cup of tea would be nice."

She glanced up at him, surprised by his choice. There was no need to mention since that first day when he'd shown up she had picked up a couple bottles of beer and wine at the store to give him more of a choice. Since tea was also her choice she said, "All right, I'll be back in a moment." She then swept from the room.

Jason watched her leave and felt more frustrated than ever. She was right, they needed to talk. He shook his head. When had things between them gotten so complicated? Had it all started with that kiss? A kiss that was destined to happen sooner or later given the intense attraction between them?

He sighed deeply, wondering how he would explain his coldness to her tonight. How could he tell her his behavior had been put in place as a safety mechanism stemming from the fact that he wanted her more than he'd ever wanted any other woman? And how could he explain that the thought of any woman getting under his skin to the extent she had scared the hell out of him?

Chances were if he hadn't run into her at the appliance store he would have sought out her company anyway. More than likely he would have dropped by later for tea, although he had tried limiting his visits for fear of wearing out his welcome.

Her phone rang and he wondered who would be calling her at this late hour but knew it was none of his business when she picked it up on the second rang. He'd never gotten around to asking if she had a boyfriend or not and assumed she didn't.

Moments later Jason glanced toward the kitchen door when he heard a loud noise, the sound of something crashing on her floor. He quickly moved toward the kitchen to see what had happened and to make sure she was all right.

He frowned when he entered the kitchen and saw Bella stooping to pick up the tray she'd dropped along with two broken cups.

He quickly moved forward. "Are you okay, Bella?" he asked.

She didn't look at him as she continued to pick up broken pieces of the teacups. "I'm fine. I accidentally dropped it."

He bent down toward her. "That's fine. At least you didn't have tea in the cups. You could have burned yourself. I can help you get that up."

She turned to look up at him. "I can do this, Jason. I don't need your help."

He met her gaze and would have taken her stinging words to heart if he hadn't seen the redness of her eyes. "What's wrong?"

Instead of answering she shook her head and averted her gaze, refusing to look at him any longer. Quickly recovering his composure at seeing her so upset, he was pushed into action and wrapped his arms around her waist and assisted her up off the floor.

He stood facing her and drew in a deep, calming breath before saying, "I want to know what's wrong, Bella."

She drew in her own deep breath. "That was my father. He called to gloat."

Jason frowned. "About what?"

He watched her when she swallowed deeply. "He and his attorney were able to get an injunction against my trust fund and wanted me to know my monthly funds are on hold."

He heard the tremor in her voice. "But I thought you had three months before your twenty-sixth birthday."

"I do, but some judge—probably a close friend of Dad's—felt my parents had grounds to place a hold on my money. They don't believe I'll marry before the trust fund's deadline date."

She frowned. "I need my money, Jason. I was counting on the income to pay my men as well as to pay for all the work I've ordered to be done around here. There were a number of things my grandfather hadn't taken care of around here that need to be done, like repairing the roof on the barn. My parents are deliberately placing me in a bind and they know it."

Jason nodded. He had started noticing a number of things Herman had begun overlooking that had needed to be done. He then shook his head. He'd heard of controlling parents but felt hers were ridiculous.

"Certainly there is something your attorney can do."

She drew in a deep breath. "He sent me a text moments ago and said there's nothing he can do now that a judge has gotten involved. And even if there were, it would take time and my parents know it. It is time they figure I don't have, which will work in their favor. True, I got this ranch free and clear but it takes money to keep it operational."

He shook his head. "And all because you won't get married?"

"Yes. They believe I was raised and groomed to be the wife of someone like Hugh who already has standing in Savannah's upper-class society."

Jason didn't say anything for a few moments. "Does your trust fund specifically state who you're to marry?"

"No, it just says I have to be a married woman. I guess my grandparents figured in their way of thinking that I would automatically marry someone they would consider my equal and not just anyone."

An idea suddenly slammed into Jason's head. It was a crazy one…but it would serve a purpose in the long run. In the end, she would get what she wanted and he would get what he wanted.

He reached out and took her hand in his, entwined their fingers and tried ignoring the sensations touching her caused. "Let's sit down for a moment. I might have an idea."

Bella allowed him to lead her over to the kitchen table and she sat down with her hands on top of the table and glanced up at him expectantly.

"Promise you'll keep an open mind when you hear my proposal."

"All right, I promise."

He paused a moment and then said, "I think you should do what your parents want and get married."

"What!"

"Think about it, Bella. You can marry anyone to keep your trust fund intact."

He could tell she was even more confused. "I don't understand, Jason. I'm not seriously involved with anyone, so who am I supposed to marry?"

"Me."

Four

Bella's jaw dropped open. "You?"

"Yes."

She stared at Jason for a long moment and then she adamantly shook her head.

"Why would you agree to marry me?" she asked, confused.

"Think about it, Bella. It will be a win-win situation for the both of us. Marriage to me will guarantee you'll keep your trust fund rolling in without your parents' interfering. And it will give me what I want, as well, which is your land and Hercules."

Her eyes widened. "A marriage of convenience between us?"

"Yes." He could see the light shining bright in her wide-eyed innocent gaze. But then caution eased into the hazel depths.

"And you want me to give you my land as well as Hercules?"

"Co-ownership of the land and total ownership of Hercules."

Bella nibbled on her bottom lip, giving his proposal consideration while trying not to feel the disappointment trying to crowd her in. She had come here to Denver to be independent and not dependent. But what he was proposing was not how she had planned things to go. She was just learning to live on her own without her parents looking over her shoulder. She wanted her own life and now Jason was proposing that he share it. Even if it was on a temporary basis, she was going to feel her independence snatched away. "And how long do we have to remain married?"

"For as long as we want but at least a year. Anytime after that either of us are free to file for a divorce to end things. But think about it, once we send your father's attorney proof we're officially married he'll have no choice but to release the hold on your trust fund."

Bella knew that her parents would always be her parents and although she loved them, she could not put up with their controlling ways any longer. She thought Jason's proposal might work but she still had a few reservations and concerns.

"Will we live in separate households?" she decided to ask.

"No, we will either live here or at my place. I have no problem moving in here but we can't live apart. We don't want to give your parents or anyone a reason to think our marriage isn't the real thing."

She nodded thinking what he said made sense but she needed to ask another question. This one was of a delicate nature but was one she definitely needed to know the answer to. She cleared her throat. "If we lived in the same house would you expect for us to sleep in the same bed?"

He held her gaze intently. "I think by now it's apparent we're attracted to each other, which is the reason I wasn't Mr. Congeniality tonight as you've indicated. That kiss we shared only made me want more and I think you know where wanting more would have led."

Yes, she knew. And because he was being honest with her she might as well be honest with him. "And the reason I acted 'cold' as you put it was that I felt sensations kissing you that I'd never felt before and with everything going on in my life, the last thing I needed to take on was a lover. And now you want me to take on a husband, Jason?"

"Yes, and only because you won't have all those issues you had before. And I would want us to share a bed, but I'll leave the decision of what we do up to you. I won't rush you into doing anything you're not comfortable with doing. But I think you can rightly say with us living under the same roof such a thing is bound to happen eventually."

She swallowed. Yes, she could rightly say that. Marrying him would definitely be a solution to her problem and like he'd said, he would be getting what he wanted out of the deal as well—co-ownership of her land and Hercules. It would be a win-win situation.

But still.

"I need to think about it, Jason. Your proposal sounds good but I need to make sure it's the right answer."

He nodded. "I have an attorney who can draw up the papers so you won't have to worry about everything I'm proposing being legit and binding. Your attorney can look at them as well if you'd like. He will be bound by attorney-client privilege not to disclose the details of our marriage to anyone."

"I still need time to think things through, Jason."

"And I'll give you that time but my proposal won't be out there forever."

"I understand."

And whether or not he believed her, she *did* understand, which was why she needed time to think about it. From his standpoint things probably looked simple and easy. But to her there were several "what ifs" she had to consider.

What if during that year she fell in love with him but he wanted out of the marriage? What if he was satisfied with a loveless marriage and like her parents wanted to be discreet in taking lovers? What if—

"How much time do you think you'll need to think about it?"

"No more than a week at the most. I should have my answer to you by then." And she hoped more than anything it would be the right one.

"All right, that will work for me."

"And you're not involved with anyone?" she asked, needing to know for certain.

He smiled. "No, I'm not. Trust me. I couldn't be involved with anyone and kiss you the way I did the other day."

Bringing up their kiss made her remember how it had been that day, and how easily her lips had molded to his. It had been so easy to feel his passion, and some of the things his tongue had done inside her mouth nearly short-circuited her brain. Even now her body was inwardly shuddering with the force of those memories. And she expected them to live under the same roof and not share a bed? That was definitely an unrealistic expectation

on her part. It seemed since their kiss, being under the
same roof for any period of time was a passionate time
bomb waiting to happen for them and they both knew
it.

She glanced across the table at him and her stomach
clenched. He was looking at her the same way he'd done
that day right before he'd kissed her. And she'd kissed
him back. Mated with his mouth and loved every minute
doing so.

Even now she recognized the look in his eyes. It was a
dark, hungry look that did more than suggest he wanted
her and if given the chance he would take her right here,
on her kitchen table. And it would entail more than just
kissing. He would probably want to sample her the same
way she'd done the seafood bisque Pam had served at
dinner. And heaven help her but she would just love to
be sampled.

She knew what he wanted but was curious to know
what he was thinking at this moment. He was staring
at her with such intensity, such longing and such greed.
Then she thought, maybe it was best that she didn't
know. It would be safer to just imagine.

Swallowing hard, she broke eye contact with him
and thought changing the subject was a good idea. The
discussion of a possible marriage between them was not
the way to go right now.

"At least I've paid for the appliances they are deliv-
ering next week," she said, glancing over at her stove that
had seen better days. "I think that stove and refrigerator
were here when my Dad lived here," she added.

"Probably."

"So it was time for new ones, don't you think?"

"Yes. And I think we need to get those broken pieces
of the teacups off the floor," he said.

"I'll do it later. It will give me something to do after you leave. I'm going to need to stay busy for a while. I'm not sleepy."

"You sure you won't need my help cleaning it up?"

"Yes, I'm sure" was her response.

"All right."

"I have beer in the refrigerator if you'd like one," she offered.

"No, I'm straight."

For the next ten minutes they continued to engage in idle chatter. Anything else was liable to set off sparks that could ignite into who knows what.

"Bella?"

"Yes."

"It's not working."

She knew just what he meant. They had moved the conversation from her appliances, to the broken teacups, to him not wanting a beer, to the furniture in her living room, to the movie that had made number one at the box office last weekend like either of them really gave a royal flip. "It's not?"

"No. It's okay to feel what we're feeling right now, no matter what decision you make a week from now. And on that note," he said, standing, "if you're sure you don't want me to help clean up the broken teacups, I think I'd better go before…"

"Before what?" she asked when he hesitated in completing the statement.

"Before I try eating you alive."

She sucked in a quick breath while a vision of him doing that very thing filtered through her mind. And then instead of leaving well enough alone, she asked something really stupid. "Why would you want to do something like that?"

He smiled. And the way he smiled had her pulse beating rapidly in several areas of her body. It wasn't a predatory smile but one of those "if you really want to know" smiles. Never before had she been aware of the many smiles a person's lips could convey.

In truth, with the little experience she had when it came to men, she was surprised she could read him at all. But for some strange reason she could read Jason and she could do so on a level that could set off passion fizzing to life inside of her.

Like it was doing now.

"The reason I'd try eating you alive is that the other day I only got a sample of your taste. But it was enough to give me plenty of sleepless nights since then. Now I find that I crave knowing how you taste all over. So if you're not ready for that to happen, come on and walk me to the door."

Honestly, at that moment she wasn't quite sure what she was ready for and figured that degree of uncertainty was reason to walk him to the door. She had a lot to think about and work out in her mind and only a week to do it.

She stood and moved around the table. When he extended his hand to her, she knew if they were to touch it would set off a chain of emotions and events she wasn't sure she was ready for. Her gaze moved away from his hand up to his face and she had a feeling that he knew it, as well. Was this supposed to be a challenge? Or was it merely a way to get her to face the facts of how living under the same roof with him would be?

She could ignore his outstretched hand but doing so would be rude and she wasn't a rude person. He was watching her. Waiting for her next move. So she made it and placed her hand in his. And the instant their hands touched she felt it. The heat of his warmth spread through her and instead of withstanding it she was drawn deeper and deeper into it.

Before she realized his intentions he let go of her hand to slide his fingertips up and down her arm in a caress so light and so mind-bogglingly sensual that she had to clamp down her mouth to keep from moaning.

The look in the dark eyes staring at her was intense and she knew at that moment his touch wasn't the only thing making her come apart. His manly scent was flowing through her nostrils and drawing him to her in a way that was actually making her panties wet.

My goodness.

"Maybe my thinking is wrong, Bella," he said in a deep, husky voice as his fingers continued to caress her arms, making her stomach clench with every heated stroke against her skin.

"Maybe you are ready for me to taste you all over, let my tongue glide across your skin, sample you in my mouth and feast on you with the deep hunger I need assuaged. And while your delicious taste sinks into my mouth, I will use my tongue to push you over the edge time and time again and drown you in a need that I intend to fulfill."

His words were pushing her over the edge just as much as his touch was doing. They were making her feel things. Want things. And increasing her desire to explore. To experience. To exert her freedom this way.

"Tell me you're ready," he urged softly in a heated voice. "Just looking at you makes me hot and hard," he said in a tone that heated her skin. "So please tell me you're ready for me."

Bella thought Jason's words had been spoken in the huskiest whisper she'd ever heard, and they did something to her both physically and mentally. They prodded her to want whatever it was he was offering. Whatever she was supposed to be ready for.

Like other women, sex was no great mystery to her. At least not since she had seen her parents' housekeeper Carlie have sex with the gardener when she was twelve. She hadn't understood at the time what all the moans and groans were about and why they had to be naked while making them. As she got older she'd been shielded from any encounters with the opposite sex and never had time to dwell on such matters.

But there had been a time when she'd become curious so she had begun reading a lot. Her parents would probably die of shame if they knew about all the romance novels Carlie would sneak in to her. It was there between the pages of those novels that she began to dream, fantasize and hope that one day she would fall in love and live happily ever after like the women she read about. Her most ardent desire was to one day find the one man who would make her sexually liberated. She wouldn't press her luck and hold out for love.

She swallowed deeply as she gazed up at Jason, knowing he was waiting for her response, and she knew at that moment what it would be. "Yes, Jason, I'm ready."

He didn't say anything for the longest time; he just stood there and stared at her. For a moment she wondered if he'd heard her. But his darkened eyes, the sound of his breathing alerted her that he had. And his eyes then traveled down the length of her throat and she knew he saw how erratically her pulse was throbbing there at the center.

And then before she could blink, he lowered his head to kiss her. His tongue drove between her lips at the same time his hand reached under her wrap dress. While his tongue relentlessly probed her mouth, his fingers began sliding up her thighs and the feel of his hands on that part of her, a part no other man had touched, made something inside of her uncoil and she released a breathless sigh. She knew at that moment the heat was on. Before she realized he'd done so, he had inched her backward and the cheeks of her behind aligned with the table.

He withdrew his mouth from hers long enough to whisper, "I can't wait to get my tongue inside of you."

His words sent all kinds of sensations swirling around in her stomach and a deep ache began throbbing between her legs. The heat was not just on, it was almost edging out of control. She felt it emitting even more when his fingers moved from her thighs to her panties.

And when he reclaimed her mouth again she moaned at how thoroughly he was kissing her and thinking her brain would overload from all the sensations ramming through her. She tried keeping up as his tongue did a methodical sweep of her mouth. And when she finally thought her senses were partially back under control, he proved her wrong when his fingers wiggled their way beneath the waistband of her panties to begin stroking her in a way that all but obliterated her senses.

"Jason…"

She felt her body being eased back onto the table at the same time her dress was pushed up to her waist. She was too full of emotions, wrapped up in way too many sensations, to take stock in what he was doing, but she got a pretty good idea when he eased her panties down her legs, leaving her open and bare to his sight. And when he eased her back farther on the table and placed her legs over his shoulders to nearly wrap around his neck she knew.

Her breath quickened at the smile that then touched his lips, a smile like before that was not predatory and this time wasn't even one of those "if you really want to know" smiles. This one was a "you're going to enjoy this" smile that curved the corners of his mouth and made a hidden dimple appear in his right cheek.

And before she could release her next breath he lifted her hips to bury his face between her legs. She bit her tongue to keep from screaming when his hot tongue slid between her womanly folds.

She squirmed frantically beneath his mouth as he drove her crazy with passion, using his tongue to coax her into the kind of climax she'd only read about. It was the kind that had preclimactic sensations rushing through her. He shoved his tongue deeper inside her, doing more than tasting her dewy wetness; he was using the hot tip of his tongue to greedily lick her from core to core.

She threw her head back and closed her eyes, as his tongue began making all kinds of circles inside her, teasing her flesh, branding it. But he wouldn't let up and she saw he had no intentions of doing so. She felt the buildup right there at the center of her thighs where his mouth was. Pleasure and heat were taking their toll.

Then suddenly her body convulsed around his mouth and she released a moan from deep within her throat as sharp jolts of sexual pleasure set ripples off in her body. And she moaned while the aftershocks made her body shudder uncontrollably. What she was enduring was unbearably erotic, pleasure so great she thought she would pass out from it.

But she couldn't pass out, not when his tongue continued to thrust inside her, forcing her to give even more. And then she was shoved over the edge. Unable to take anymore, she tightened her legs around his neck and cried out in ecstasy as waves after turbulent waves overtook her.

It was only when the last spasm had eased from her body did he tear his mouth away from her, lower her legs, lean down and kiss her, letting her taste the essence of herself from his lips.

She sucked hard on his tongue, needing it like a lifeline and knowing at that moment he had to be the most sensual and passionate man to walk on the planet. He had made her feel things she'd never felt before, far greater than what she had imagined in any of those romance novels. And she knew this was just the beginning, an introduction to what was out there... and she had a feeling of what was to come.

She knew at that moment, while their tongues continued to mate furiously, that after tonight there was no way they could live under the same roof and not want to discover what was beyond this. How far into pleasure could he take her?

She was definitely going to have to give the proposal he'd placed out there some serious thought.

Jason eased Bella's dress back down her thighs before lifting her from the table to stand on her feet. He studied her features and was pleased with what he saw. Her eyes glowed, her lips were swollen and she looked well rested when she hadn't slept.

But more than anything he thought she was the most beautiful woman he'd ever seen. He hoped he'd given her something to think about, something to anticipate, because more than anything he wanted to marry her.

He intended to marry her.

"Come on, walk me to the door," he whispered thickly. "And this time I promise to leave."

He took her hand in his and ignored the sensations he felt whenever he touched her. "Have breakfast with me tomorrow."

She glanced up at him. "You don't intend to make my decision easy, do you?"

A soft chuckle escaped his lips. "Nothing's wrong with me giving you something to think about. To remember. And to anticipate. It will only help you to make the right decision about my proposal."

When they reached her door he leaned down and kissed her again. She parted her lips easily for him and he deepened the kiss, finding her tongue and then enjoying a game of hide-and-seek with it before finally releasing her mouth on a deep, guttural moan. "What about breakfast in the morning at my place?" he asked huskily.

"That's all it's going to be, right? Breakfast and nothing more?" she asked, her voice lower than a whisper.

He smiled at her with a mischievous grin on his face. "We'll see."

"In that case I'll pass. I can't take too much of you, Jason Westmoreland."

He laughed as he pulled her closer into his arms. "Sweetheart, if I have my way, one of these days you're going to take *all* of me." He figured she knew just what he meant with his throbbing erection all but poking at her center. Maybe she was right and for them to share breakfast tomorrow wasn't a good idea. He would be pouncing on her before she got inside his house.

"A rain check, then?" he prompted.

"Um, maybe."

He lifted a brow. "You're not trying to play hard to get, are you?"

She smiled. "You can ask me that after what happened a short while ago in my kitchen? But I will warn you that I intend to build up some type of immunity to your charms by the time I see you again. You can be overwhelming, Jason."

He chuckled again, thinking she hadn't seen anything yet. Leaning over he brushed a kiss across her lips. "Think about me tonight, Bella."

He opened the door and walked out, thinking the next seven days were bound to be the longest he'd ever endured.

Later that night Bella couldn't get to sleep. Her body was tingling all over from the touch of a man. But it hadn't been any man, it had been Jason. When she tried closing her eyes all she could see was how it had been in her kitchen, the way Jason had draped her across the table and proceeded to enjoy her in such a scandalous way. The nuns at her school would have heart failure to know what had happened to her…and to know how much she had enjoyed it.

All her life she'd been taught—it had virtually been drilled into her head—all about the sins of the flesh. It was wrong for a woman to engage in any type of sexual encounter with a man before marriage. But how could something be so wrong if it felt so right?

Color tinted her cheeks. She needed to get to Confessions the first chance she got. She'd given in to temptation tonight and as much as she had enjoyed it, it would be something she couldn't repeat. Those kinds of activities belonged to people who were married and doing otherwise was improper.

She was just going to have to make sure she and Jason weren't under the same roof alone for a long period of time. Things could get out of hand. She was a weakling when it came to him. He would tempt her to do things she knew she shouldn't.

And now she was paying the price for her little indulgence by not being able to get to sleep. There was no doubt in her mind that Jason's mouth should be outlawed. She inwardly sighed. It was going to take a rather long time to clear those thoughts from her mind.

Five

"I like Bella, Jason."

He glanced over at his cousin Zane. It was early Monday morning and they were standing in the round pen with one of the mares while waiting for Derringer to bring the designated stallion from his stall for the scheduled breeding session. "I like her, too."

Zane chuckled. "Could have fooled me. Because you weren't giving her your attention at dinner Friday night. We all felt that it was up to us to make her feel welcome, because you were ignoring the poor girl."

Jason rolled his eyes. "And I bet it pained all of you to do so."

"Not really. Your Southern Bella is a real classy lady. If you weren't interested in her I'd make a play for her."

"But I *am* interested in her."

"I know," Zane said, smiling. "It was pretty obvious. I

intercepted your dirty looks loud and clear. In any case, I hope things get straightened out between you two."

"I hope so, too. I'll find out in five more days."

Zane lifted a curious brow. "Five days? What's supposed to happen in five days?"

"Long story and one which I prefer not to share right now." He had intentionally not contacted Bella over the past two days to give her breathing space from him to think his proposal through. He'd thought it through and it made perfect sense to him. He was beginning to anticipate her answer. It would be yes; it just had to be.

But what if yes wasn't her answer? What if even after the other night and the sample lovemaking they'd shared that she thought his proposal wasn't worth taking the chance? He would be the first to admit that his proposal was a bit daring. But he felt the terms were fair. Hell, he was giving her a chance to be the first to file for a divorce after the first year. And he—

Zane snapped a finger in front of his face. "Hellooo. Are you with us? Derringer is here with Fireball. Are you up to this or are you thinking about mating of another kind?" Zane was grinning.

Jason frowned when he glanced over at Derringer and saw a smirk on his face, as well. "Yes, I'm up to this and it's none of your business what I'm thinking about."

"Fine, just keep Prancer straight while Fireball mounts her. It's been a while since he's had a mare and he might be overly eager," Zane said with a meaningful smile.

Just like me, Jason thought, remembering every vivid detail of Bella spread out on her kitchen table for him to enjoy. "All right, let's get this going. I have something to do later."

Both Zane and Derringer gave him speculative looks but said nothing.

* * *

Bella stepped out of the shower and began toweling herself dry. It was the middle of the day but after going for a walk around the ranch she had gotten hot and sticky. Now she intended to slip into something comfortable and have a cup of tea and relax…and think about Jason's proposal.

The walk had done her good and walking her land had made her even more determined to hold on to what was hers. But was Jason's proposal the answer? Or would she be jumping out of the pot and into the fire?

After Friday night and what had gone down in her kitchen, there was no doubt in her mind that Jason was the kind of lover women dreamed of having. And he had to be the most unselfish person she knew. He had given her pleasure without seeking his own. She had read enough articles on the subject to know most men weren't usually that generous. But he had been and her body hadn't been the same since. Every time she thought about him and that night in the kitchen, she had to pause and catch her breath.

She hadn't heard from him since that night but figured he was giving her time to think things through before she gave him her answer. She had talked to her attorney again and he hadn't said anything to make her think she had a chance of getting the hold on her trust fund lifted.

She had run into her uncle yesterday when she'd gone into town and he hadn't been at all pleasant. And neither had his son, daughter and two teenage grandsons. All of them practically cut her with their sharp looks. She just didn't get it. Jason had wanted her land as well but he hadn't been anything but supportive of her decision to keep it and had offered his help from the first.

She understood that she and her Denver relatives didn't have the same bond as the Westmorelands but she would think they wouldn't be dismissing her the way they were doing over some land.

She had dressed and was heading downstairs when something like a missile sailed through her living room window, breaking the glass in the process. "What on earth!" She nearly missed her step when she raced back up the stairs to her bedroom, closing the door and locking it behind her.

Catching her breath she grabbed her cell phone off the nightstand and called the police.

"Where is she, Marvin?" Jason asked, walking into Bella's house with Zane and Derringer on his heels.

"She's in the kitchen," the man answered, moving quickly out of Jason's way.

Jason had gotten a call from Pam to tell him what had happened. He had jumped in his truck and left Zane's ranch immediately with Derringer and Zane following close behind in their vehicles.

From what Pam had said, someone had thrown a large rock through Bella's window with a note tied to it saying, "Go back to where you came from." The thought of anyone doing that angered him. Who on earth would do such a thing?

He walked into the kitchen and glanced around, dismissing memories of the last time he'd been there and his focus immediately went to Bella. She was sitting at the kitchen table talking to Pete Higgins, one of the sheriff's deputies and a good friend of Derringer's.

Everyone glanced up when he entered and the look on Bella's face was like a kick in his gut. He could tell she was shaken and there was a hurt expression in her eyes he'd never seen before. His anger flared at the thought that someone could hurt her in any way. The rock may not have hit her but she'd taken a hit just the same. Whoever had thrown that rock through the window had hit her spirit and left her shaken.

"Jason, Zane and Derringer," Pete said, acknowledging their arrival. "Why am I not surprised to see the three of you here?"

Jason didn't respond as he moved straight toward Bella and, disregarding the onlookers, he reached out to caress the soft skin beneath her ear. "Are you all right?" he whispered in a husky tone.

She held his gaze and nodded slowly. "Yes, I'm fine. I was on my way downstairs when that rock came flying through the window. It scared me more than anything."

He glanced at the rock that someone had placed on the table. It was a huge rock, big enough to hurt her had she been in her living room anywhere near the window. The thought of anyone harming one single hair on her head infuriated him.

He glanced over at Pete. "Do you have any idea who did it?"

Peter shook his head. "No, but both the rock and note have been dusted for fingerprints. Hopefully we'll know something soon."

Soon? He wanted to know something now. He glanced down at the note and read it.

"I was just asking Ms. Bostwick if she knew of anyone who wanted her off this property. The only people she could think of are her parents and possibly Kenneth Bostwick."

"I can't see my parents behind anything like this," Bella said in a soft voice. "And I don't want to think

Uncle Kenneth is capable of doing anything like this, either. However, he does want me off the land because he knows of someone who wants to buy it."

Pete nodded. "What about Jason here? I think we all know he wants your land and Hercules, as well," the deputy said as if Jason wasn't standing right there listening to his every word. "Do you think he'd want you gone, too?"

Bella seemed surprised by the question and moved her gaze from Pete to Jason. Jason figured she saw remnants of passion behind the anger in his eyes.

"No, he'd want me to stay," she said with a soft sigh.

Pete closed his notepad, evidently deciding not to ask why she was so certain of that. "Well, hopefully we'll have something within a week if those fingerprints are identified," he said.

"And what is she supposed to do in the meantime, Pete?" Jason asked in a frustrated tone.

"Report anything suspicious," Pete responded dryly. He turned to face Bella. "I'll request that the sheriff beef up security around here starting today."

"Thank you, Deputy Higgins," Bella said softly. "I'd appreciate that tremendously. Marvin is getting the window replaced and I'll be keeping the lights on in the yard all night now."

"Doesn't matter," Jason said. "You're staying at my place tonight."

Bella tilted her head to the side and met Jason's intense gaze. "I can't do that. You and I can't stay under the same roof."

Jason crossed his arms over his chest. "And why not?"

A flush stole into her cheeks when she noted Jason

wasn't the only one waiting on her response. "You know why," she finally said.

Jason's forehead bunched up. Then when he re-membered what could possibly happen if they stayed overnight under the same roof, he smiled. "Oh, yeah."

"Oh, yeah, what?" Zane wanted to know.

Jason frowned at his cousin. "None of your busi-ness."

Pete cleared his throat. "I'm out of here but like I said, Miss Bostwick, the department will have more police checking around the area." He slipped both the rock and note into a plastic evidence bag.

Zane and Derringer followed Pete out the door, which Jason appreciated since it gave him time alone with Bella. The first thing he did was lean down and kiss her. He needed the taste of her to know she was really okay.

She responded to his kiss and automatically he deepened it, drawing her up out of the chair to stand on her feet in the process. He needed the feel of all of her to know she was safe. He would protect her with his life if he had to. He'd aged a good twenty years when he'd gotten that call from Pam telling him what had happened. And speaking of Pam's phone call…

He broke off the kiss and with an irritated frown on his features he looked down at Bella. "Why didn't you call me? Why did I have to hear what happened from someone else?"

She gazed right back at him with an irritated frown of her own. "You've never given me your phone num-ber."

Jason blinked in surprise and realized what she'd said was true. He hadn't given her his phone number.

"I apologize for that oversight," he said. "You will

definitely have it from here on out. And we need to talk about you moving in with me for a while."

She shook her head. "I can't move in with you, Jason, and as I said earlier, we both know why."

"Do you honestly think if you gave me an order not to touch you that I wouldn't keep my hands off you?" he asked.

She shrugged delicate shoulders. "Yes, I believe you'd do as I ask, but I'm not sure given that same scenario, in light of what happened in this very kitchen Friday night, that I'd be able to keep my hands off you."

He blinked. Stared down at her and blinked again. This time with a smile on his lips. "You don't say?"

"I do say and I know it's an awful thing to admit, but right now I can't make you any promises," she said, rubbing her hands together as if distressed by the very notion.

He wasn't distressed, not even a little bit. In fact, he was elated. For a minute he couldn't say a word and then said, "And you think I have a problem with you not being able to keep your hands off me?"

She nodded. "If you don't have a problem with it then you should. We aren't married. We aren't even engaged."

"I asked you to marry me Friday night."

She used her hand to wave off his reminder. "Yes, but it would be a marriage of convenience, which I haven't agreed to yet since the issue of the sleeping arrangements is still up in the air. Until I do decide I think it's best if you stay under your roof and I stay under mine. Yes, that's the proper thing to do."

He lifted a brow. "The proper thing to do?"

"Yes, proper, appropriate, suitable, fitting, which of those words do you prefer using?"

"What about none of them?"

"It doesn't matter, Jason. It's bad enough that we got carried away the other night in this kitchen. But we can't repeat something like that."

He didn't see why they couldn't and was about to say as much when he heard footsteps approaching and glanced over as Derringer and Zane entered the kitchen.

"Pete thinks he's found a footprint outside near the bushes and is checking it out now," Derringer informed them.

Jason nodded. He then turned back to Bella and his expression was one that would accept no argument on the matter. "Pack an overnight bag, Bella. You're staying at my place tonight even if I have to sleep in the barn."

Six

Bella glared at Jason. It was a ladylike glare but a glare nonetheless. She opened her mouth to say something then remembered they had an audience and immediately closed it. She cast a warm smile over at Zane and Derringer. "I'd like a few minutes alone with Jason to discuss a private matter, please."

They returned her smile, nodded and gave Jason "you've done it now" smiles before walking out of the kitchen.

It was then that she turned her attention back to Jason. "Now then, Jason, let's not be ridiculous. You are not sleeping in your barn just so I can sleep under your roof. I'm staying right here."

She could tell he did not appreciate his order not being obeyed when she saw his irritation with her increase. "Have you forgotten someone threw a rock through your window with a note demanding you leave town?"

She nibbled a minute on her bottom lip. "No, I didn't forget the rock or the note attached to it, but I can't let them think they've won by running away. I admit to being a little frightened at first but I'm fine now. Marvin is having the window replaced and I'll keep lights shining around here all night. And don't forget Marvin sleeps in the bunkhouse each night so technically, I won't be here by myself. I'll fine but I appreciate your concern."

Jason stared at her for a moment and didn't say anything. He hadn't lied about aging twenty years when he'd gotten that call from Pam. He had walked into her house not knowing what to expect. The thought that someone wanted her gone bothered him, because he knew she wasn't going anywhere and that meant he needed to protect her.

"Fine, you stay inside here and I'll sleep in your barn," he finally said.

She shook her head after crossing her arms over her chest. "You won't be sleeping in anyone's barn. You're going to sleep in your own bed tonight and I intend to sleep in mine."

"Fine," he snapped like he was giving in to her suggestion when he wouldn't do anything of the sort. But if she wanted to think it he would let her. "I need to take you to Pam's to show her and the others you're okay and in one piece."

A smile touched her lips. "They were worried about me?"

She seemed surprised by that. "Yes, everyone was worried."

"In that case let me grab my purse."

"I'll be waiting outside," he said to her fleeing back.

He shook his head and slowly left the kitchen and walked through the dining room to the living room where Marvin and a couple of the men were replacing the window. They had cleaned up all the broken glass but a scratch mark on the wooden floor clearly showed where the rock had landed once it entered the house.

He drew in a sharp breath at the thought of Bella getting hit by that rock. If anything would have happened to her he would have...

At that moment he wasn't sure just what he would do. The thought of anything happening to her sent sharp fear through him in a way he'd never known before. Why? Why were his feelings for her so intense? Why was he so possessive when it came to her?

He shrugged off the responses that flowed through his mind, not ready to deal with any of them. He walked out the front door to where Zane and Derringer were waiting.

"You aren't really going to let her stay here unprotected?" Derringer asked, studying his features.

Jason shook his head. "No."

"And why can't the two of you stay under the same roof?" Zane asked curiously.

"None of your business."

Zane chuckled. "If you don't give me an answer I'm going to think things."

That didn't move Jason. "Think whatever you want." He then checked his watch. "I hate to do this but I'm checking out for the rest of the day. I intend to keep an eye on Bella until Pete finds out who threw that rock through her window."

"You think Kenneth Bostwick had something to do with it?" Derringer asked.

"Not sure, but I hope for his sake he didn't," Jason said in a voice laced with tightly controlled anger.

He stopped talking when Bella walked onto the porch. Not only had she grabbed her purse but she'd also changed her dress. At his curious look, she said, "The dress I was wearing wasn't suitable for visiting."

He nodded and decided not to tell her she looked good now and had looked good then. Whatever she put on her body she wore with both grace and style. He met her in the middle of the porch and slipped her hand in his. "You look nice. And I thought we could grab dinner someplace before I bring you back here."

Her eyes glowed in a way that tightened his stomach and sent sensations rushing through his gut. "I'd like that, Jason."

It was close to ten at night when Bella returned home. Jason entered her house and checked around, turning on lights as he went from room to room. It made her feel extra safe when she saw a police patrol car parked near the turnoff to her property.

"Everything looks okay," Jason said, breaking into her thoughts.

"Thanks. I'll walk you to the door," she said quickly, heading back downstairs.

"Trying to rush me out of here, Bella?"

At the moment she didn't care what he thought. She just needed him gone so she could get her mind straightened out. Being with him for the past eight hours had taken its toll on her mind and body.

She hadn't known he was so touchy and each time he'd touched her, even by doing something simple as placing a hand in the center of her back when they'd been walking into the movies, it had done something to her in a way that had her hot and bothered for the rest of the evening.

But she had enjoyed the movies they'd gone to after dinner. She had enjoyed sitting beside him while he held her hand when he wasn't feeding her popcorn.

"No, I'm not trying to rush you, Jason, but it is late," she said. "If your goal this evening was to tire me out then you've done a good job of it. I plan to take a shower and then go to bed."

They were standing facing each other and he wrapped his arms around her and took a step closer, almost plastering his body to hers. She could feel all of him from chest to knee; but especially the erect body part in between.

"I'd love to take a shower with you, sweetheart," he whispered.

She didn't know what he was trying to do, but he'd been whispering such naughty come-ons to her all evening. And each and every one of them had only added to her torment. "Taking a shower together wouldn't be right, Jason, and you know it."

He chuckled. "Trying to send me home to an empty bed isn't right, either. Why don't you just accept my proposal? We can get married the same day. No waiting. And then," he said, leaning closer to begin nibbling around her mouth, "we can sleep under the same roof that night. Just think about that."

Bella moaned against the onslaught of his mouth on hers. She was thinking about it and could just imagine it. Oh, what a night that would be. But then she also had to think about what would happen if he got tired of her like her father had eventually gotten tired of her mother. The way her mother had gotten tired of her father. What if he approached her about wanting an open marriage?

What if he told her after the first year that he wanted a divorce and she'd gotten attached to him? She could just imagine the heartbreak she would feel.

"Bella?"

She glanced up at him. "Yes?"

Jason Westmoreland was such a handsome man that it made her heart ache. And at the same time he made parts of her sizzle in desire so thick you could cut it with a knife. She thought his features were flawless and he had to have the most irresistible pair of lips born to any man. Staring at his mouth pushed her to recall the way their tongues would entangle in his mouth while they mated them like crazy. It didn't take much to wonder how things would be between them in the bedroom. But she knew as tempting as it was, there was more to a marriage than just great sex. But could she really ask for more from a marriage of convenience?

"Are you sure you don't want me to stay tonight? I could sleep on the sofa."

She shook her head. Even that would be too close for comfort for her. "No, Jason, I'll be fine. Go home."

"Not before I do this," he said, leaning down and capturing her mouth with his. She didn't have a problem offering him what he wanted and he proved he didn't have a problem taking it. He kissed her deeply, thoroughly and with no reservations about making her feel wanted, needed and desired. She could definitely feel heat radiating from his body to hers and wasn't put off by it. Instead it ignited passion within her so acute she had to fight to keep a level head or risk the kiss taking them places she wasn't ready to go.

Moments later she was the one who broke off the kiss. Desperately needing to breathe, she inhaled a deep breath. Jason just simply stood there staring and waiting, as if he was ready to go another round.

Bella knew she disappointed him when she took a step back. "Good night, Jason."

His lips curved into a too-sexy smile. "Tell me one thing that will be good about it once I walk out that door."

She really wasn't sure what she could say to that and in those cases she'd always been told it was better not to say anything at all. Instead she repeated herself while turning the knob on the door to open it. "Good night, Jason.

He leaned in, brushed a kiss across her lips and whispered, "Good night, Bella."

Bella wasn't sure what brought her awake during the middle of the night. Glancing over at the clock on her nightstand she saw it was two in the morning. She was restless. She was hot. And she was definitely still bothered. She hadn't known just spending time with a man could put a woman in such an erotic state.

Sliding out of bed she slipped into her robe and house shoes. A full moon was in the sky and its light spread into the room. She was surprised by how easily sleep had come to her at first. But that had been a few hours ago and now she was wide-awake.

She moved over to the windows to look out. Under the moon-crested sky she could see the shape of the mountains in their majestic splendor. At night they were just as overpowering as they were in the daylight.

She was about to move away from the window when she happened to glance down below and saw a truck parked in her yard. She frowned and pressed her face closer to the window to make out just whose vehicle was parked in her yard and frowned when she recognized the vehicle was Jason's.

What was his truck doing in her yard at two in the morning? Was he in it?

She rushed downstairs. He couldn't be in a truck in front of her house at two in the morning. What would Marvin think? What would the police officers cruising the area think? His family?

When she made it to the living room she slowly opened the door and slipped out. She then released a disgusted sigh when she saw he was sitting in the truck. He had put his seat in a reclining position, but that had to be uncomfortable for him.

As if he'd been sleeping with one eye open and another one closed, he came awake when she rounded the truck and tapped on his window. He slowly tilted his Stetson back from covering his eyes. "Yes, Bella?"

She opened her mouth to speak and then closed it. If she thought he was a handsome man before then he was even more now with the shadow covering his jaw. There was just something ultrasexy about a man who hadn't shaved.

She fought her attention away from his jaw back to his gaze. "What are you doing here? Why did you come back?"

"I never left."

She blinked. "You never left? You mean to tell me you've been out here in the car since I walked you to the door?"

He smiled that sexy smile. "Yes, I've been here since you walked me to the door."

"But why?"

"To protect you."

That simple statement suddenly took the wind out of

her sail for just a moment. Merely a moment. That was all the time she needed to be reminded that no one had tried truly protecting her before. She'd always considered her parents' antics more in the line of controlling than protecting.

She then recovered and remembered why he couldn't sit out here protecting her. "But you can't sit out here, Jason. It's not proper. What will your family think if any of them see your car parked in front of my house at this hour? What would those policemen think? What would—"

"Honestly, Bella, I really don't give a royal damn what anyone thinks. I refuse to let you stay here without being close by to make sure you're okay. You didn't want me to sleep in the barn so this is where I am and where I will stay."

She frowned. "You're being difficult."

"No, I'm being a man looking out for the woman I want. Now go back inside and lock the door behind you. You interrupted my sleep."

She stared at him for a long moment and then said, "Fine, you win. Come on inside."

He stared back at her. "That wasn't what this was about, Bella. I recognize the fact just as much as you do that we don't need to be under the same roof alone. I'm fine with being out here tonight."

"Well, I'm not fine with it."

"Sorry about that but there's nothing I can do about it."

She glared at him and seeing he was determined to be stubborn, she threw up her hands before going back into the house, closing the door behind her.

Jason heard the lock click in place and swore he could also hear her fuming all the way up the stairs. She could fume all she wanted but he wasn't leaving. He had been sitting out there for the past four hours thinking, and the more he thought the more he realized something vital to him. And it was something he could not deny or ignore. He had fallen in love with Bella. And accepting how he felt gave his proposal much more meaning than what he'd presented to her. Now he fully understood why Derringer had acted so strangely while courting Lucia.

He had dated women in the past but had never loved any of them. He'd known better than to do so after that fiasco with Mona Cardington in high school. He'd admitted he loved her and when a new guy moved to town weeks later she had dumped him like a hot potato. That had been years ago but the pain he'd felt that day had been real and at seventeen it had been what had kept him from loving another woman.

And now he had fallen head over heels in love with a Southern belle and for the time being would keep how he felt to himself.

An hour later Bella lay in bed staring up at the ceiling, still inwardly fuming. How dare Jason put her in such a compromising position? No one would think he was sleeping in the truck. People were going to assume they were lovers and he was sleeping in her bed, lying with her between silken sheets with their limbs entwined and mouths fused while making hot, passionate and steamy love.

Her thighs began to quiver and the juncture between her legs began to ache just thinking of how it would probably be if they were to share a bed. He would stroke her senseless with his fingers in her most intimate spot first, taking his time to get her primed and ready for the next stage of what he would do to her.

She shifted to her side and held her legs tightly together, hoping the ache would go away. She'd never craved a man before and now she was craving Jason something fierce, more so than ever since he'd tasted her there. All she had to do was close her eyes and remember being stretched out on her kitchen table with his head between her legs and how he had lapped her into sweet oblivion. The memories sent jolts of electricity throughout her body, making the tips of her breasts feel sensitive against her nightgown.

And the man causing her so much torment and pleasure was downstairs sleeping in his truck just to keep her safe. She couldn't help but be touched that he would do such a thing. He had given up a nice comfortable bed and was sleeping in a position that couldn't be relaxing with his hat over his eyes to shield the brightness of the lights around her yard. Why? Was protecting her that important to him?

If it was, then why?

Deep down she knew the reason and it stemmed from him wanting her land and Hercules. He had been up-front about it from the beginning. She had respected him for it and for accepting the decision was hers to make. So, in other words, he wasn't really protecting her per se but merely protecting his interest, or what he hoped to be his interest. She figured such a thing made sense but...

Would accepting the proposal Jason placed on the table be in her best interest? Did she have a choice if she wanted the hold lifted on her trust fund? Was being legally bound to Jason as his wife for a minimum of a year something she wanted? What about sleeping under

the same roof with him and sharing his bed—she'd
accepted they would be synonymous—be in her best
interest? Was it what she wanted to do, knowing in a
year's time he could walk away without looking back?
Knowing after that time he would be free to marry
someone else? Free to make love to someone else the
same way he'd make love to her?

And then there was the question of who was
responsible for throwing the rock inside her house.
Why was someone trying to scare her off? Although
she doubted it, could it be her parents' doing to get her
to run back home?

She yawned when she felt sleep coming down on her.
Although she regretted Jason was sleeping in his truck,
she knew she could sleep a lot more peacefully knowing
he was the one protecting her.

Bella woke to the sound of someone knocking on her
door and discovered it was morning. She quickly eased
out of bed and slid into her bathrobe and bedroom shoes
to head downstairs.

"I'm coming!" she called out, rushing to the door.
She glanced out the peephole and saw it was Jason. Her
heart began beating fast and furiously in her chest at the
sight of him, handsome and unshaven with his Stetson
low on his brow. Mercy!

Taking a deep breath she opened the door. "Good
morning, Jason."

"Good morning, Bella. I wanted to let you know I'm
leaving to go home and freshen up, but Riley is here."

"Your brother Riley?" she asked, looking over his
shoulder to see the truck parked next to his and the man
sitting inside. Riley threw up his hand in a wave which
she returned. She recalled meeting him that night at

dinner. Jason was older than Riley by two and a half years.

"Yes, my brother Riley."

She was confused. "Why is he here?"

"Because I'm going home to freshen up." He tilted his head and smiled at her. "Are you awake yet?"

"Yes, I'm awake and I know you said you're going home to change but why does Riley have to be here? It's not like I need a bodyguard or something. A rock got thrown through my window, Jason. Not a scud missile."

He merely kept smiling at her while leaning in her doorway. And then he said, "Has anyone ever told you how beautiful you look in the morning?"

She stood there and stared at him. Not ready for him to change the subject and definitely not prepared for him to say something so nice about how she looked. She could definitely return the favor and ask, had anyone ever told him how handsome he looked in the morning. However, she was certain a number of women already had.

So she answered him honestly. "No one has ever told me that."

"Then let me go on record as being your first."

She drew in a deep breath. He didn't say "the" first but had said "your" first. He had made it personal and exclusive. She wondered what he would think to know she had drifted off to sleep last night with images of him flittering through her mind. Memories of his mouth on her probably elicited pleasurable sighs from her even while she slept.

"Doesn't Riley have to go to work today?" she asked, remembering when he'd mentioned that Riley worked for Blue Ridge Management. She'd even seen his name on one of the doors when they'd exited from the elevator on the fortieth floor.

"Yes, but he'll leave whenever I get back."

She crossed her arms over her chest. "And what about you? Don't you have horses to breed or train?"

"Your safety is more important to me."

"Yeah, right."

He lifted a brow. "You don't believe me? Even after I spent the entire night in my truck?"

"You were protecting your interest."

"And that's definitely you, sweetheart."

Don't even go there. Bella figured it was definitely time to end this conversation. If she engaged in chatter with him too much longer he would be convincing her that everything he was saying was true.

"You will have an answer for me in four days, right, Bella?"

"That's my plan."

"Good. I'll be back by the time you're dressed and we can do breakfast with Dillon and Pam, and then I want to show you what I do for a living."

Before she could respond he leaned in and kissed her on the lips. "See you in an hour. And wear your riding attire."

She sucked in a deep breath and watched as he walked off the porch to his truck to drive away. The man was definitely something else. She cast a quick glance to where Riley sat in his own truck sipping a cup of coffee. There was no doubt in her mind Riley had seen his brother kiss her, and she could only imagine what he was thinking.

Deciding the least she could do was invite him in, she called out to him. "You're welcome to come inside, Riley," she said, smiling broadly at him.

The smile he returned was just as expansive as he leaned his head slightly out the truck's window and said, "Thanks, but Jason warned me not to. I'm fine."

Jason warned him not to? Of course he was just joking, although he looked dead serious.

Instead of questioning him about it, she nodded, closed the door and headed back upstairs. As she entered her bedroom she couldn't ignore the excitement she felt about riding with Jason and checking out his horse training business.

Jason had grabbed his Stetson off the rack and was about to head out the door when his cell phone rang. He pulled it off his belt and saw it was Dillon.

"Yes, Dil?"

"Pam wanted me to call and verify that you and Bella are coming for breakfast."

Jason smiled. "Yes, we'll be there. In fact I'm about to saddle up one of the mares. I thought we'd ride over on horseback. We can enjoy the sights along the way."

"That's a good idea. Everything's okay at her place?"

"Yes, so far so good. The sheriff has increased the patrols around Bella's house and I appreciate it. Thank him the next time the two of you shoot pool together."

Dillon chuckled. "I will. And just so you know, I like Bella. She has a lot of class."

Jason smiled. That meant a lot coming from his older brother. While growing up he'd always thought Dillon was smart with a good head on his shoulders. Jason's admiration increased when Dillon had worked hard to keep the family together.

"And thanks, Dillon."

"For what?"

"For being you. For being there when all of us needed

you to be. For doing what you knew Mom and Dad, as well as Uncle Thomas and Aunt Susan would have wanted you to do."

"You don't have to thank me, Jason."

"Yes, I do."

Dillon didn't say anything for a moment. "Then you're welcome. Now don't keep us waiting with Bella. We won't start breakfast until the two of you get here. At least all of us except Denver. He wakes up hungry. Pam has fed him already," Dillon said.

Jason couldn't help but smile, and not for the first time, as he thought of one day having a son of his own. Being around Denver had the tendency to put such thoughts into his head. He enjoyed his nephew immensely.

"We'll get there in good time, I promise," he said before clicking off the phone.

Bella glanced down at her riding attire and smiled. She wanted to be ready when Jason returned.

Grabbing her hat off the rack she placed it on her head and opened the door to step outside on the porch. Riley had gotten out of the truck and was leaning against it. He glanced over at her and smiled.

"Ready to go riding I see," he said.

"Yes, Jason told me to be ready. We're having breakfast with Dillon and Pam."

"Yes, I had planned to have breakfast with them as well but I have a meeting at the office."

Bella nodded. "You enjoy working inside?"

Riley chuckled. "Yes, I'll leave the horses, dirt and grime to Jason. He's always liked being outdoors. When he worked at Blue Ridge I knew it was just a matter of time before wanderlust got ahold of him. He's good with horses, so are Zane and Derringer. Joining in with the Montana Westmorelands in that horse business was great for them."

Bella nodded again. "So exactly what do you do at Blue Ridge?"

"Mmm, a little bit of everything. I like to think of myself as Dillon's right-hand man. But my main job is PR. I have to make sure Blue Ridge keeps a stellar image."

Bella continued to engage in conversation with Riley while thinking he was another kind Westmoreland man. It seemed that all of them were. But she'd heard Bailey remark more than once that Riley was also a ladies' man, and she could definitely believe that. Like Jason, he was handsome to a fault.

"So, Riley, when will you settle down and get married?" she asked him, just to see what his response would be.

"Married? Me? Never. I like things just the way they are. I am definitely not the marrying kind."

Bella smiled, wondering if Jason wasn't the marrying kind, as well, although he'd given a marriage proposal to her. Did he want joint ownership of her land and Hercules that much? Evidently so.

Jason smiled as he headed back to Bella's ranch with a horse he knew she would love riding. Fancy Free was an even tempered mare. In the distance, he could see Bella was standing on the porch waiting for him. He would discount the fact that she seemed to be having an enjoyable conversation with Riley, who seemed to be flirting with her.

He ignored the signs of jealousy seeping into his bones. Riley was his brother and if you couldn't trust your own brother who could you trust? A lightbulb suddenly went off in his head. Hell. Had Abel assumed the same thing about Cain?

He tightened his hands on his horse and increased his pace to a gallop. What was Riley saying to Bella to make her laugh so much anyway? Riley was becoming a regular ladies' man around town. It seemed he was trying to keep up with Zane in that aspect. Jason had always thought Riley's playboy ways were amusing. Until now.

Moments later he brought his horse to a stop by the edge of Bella's porch. He tilted his Stetson back on his head so it wouldn't shield his eyes. "Excuse me if I'm interrupting anything."

Riley had the nerve to grin up at him. "No problem but you're twenty minutes late. You better be glad I enjoy Bella's company."

Jason frowned at his brother. "I can tell."

His gaze then shifted to Bella. She looked beautiful standing there in a pair of riding breeches that fitted her body to perfection, a white shirt and a pair of riding boots. She didn't just look beautiful, she looked hot as sin and a side glance at Riley told him that his brother was enjoying the view as much as he was.

"Don't you need to be on your way to work, Riley?"

His brother gave him another grin. "I guess so. Call if you need me as Bella's bodyguard again." He then got into his truck and pulled off.

Jason watched him leave before turning his full attention back to Bella. "Ready to go riding, sweetheart?"

As Bella rode with Jason she tried concentrating on the sheer beauty of the rustic countryside instead of the sexiness of the man in the saddle beside her. He was riding Hercules and she could tell he was an expert horseman. And she could tell why he wanted to own the stallion. It was as if he and the horse had a personal relationship. It was evident Hercules had been glad to see him. Whereas the stallion had been like putty in Jason's hands the horse had given the others grief in trying to handle him. Even now the two seemed in sync.

This was beautiful countryside and the first time she'd seen it. She was stunned by its beauty. The mare he'd chosen for her had come from his stable and was the one he'd rode over to her place. She liked how easily she and the horse were able to take the slopes that stretched out into valleys. The landscape looked majestic with the mountains in the distance.

First they rode over to Dillon and Pam's for breakfast. She had fallen in love with the Westmoreland Estate the first time she had seen it. The huge Victorian style home with a wide circular driveway sat on three hundred acres of land. Jason had told her on the ride over that as the oldest cousin, Dillon had inherited the family home. It was where most of the family seemed to congregate the majority of the time.

She had met Pam's three younger sisters the other night at dinner and enjoyed their company again around the breakfast table. Everyone asked questions about the rock throwing incident and Dillon, who knew the sheriff personally, felt the person or persons responsible would eventually get caught.

After breakfast they were in the saddle again. Jason and Bella rode to Zane's place. She was given a front row seat and watched as Zane, Derringer and Jason exercised several of the horses. Jason had explained some of the horses needed both aerobic and anaerobic training, and that so many hours each day were spent on that task. She could tell that it took a lot of skill as well as experience for any trainer to be successful and achieve the goals they wanted for the horses they trained.

At noon Lucia arrived with box lunches for everyone and Bella couldn't help noticing how much the newlyweds were still into each other. She knew if she decided to marry Jason they would not share the type of marriage Derringer and Lucia did since their union would be more of a business arrangement than anything else. But it was so obvious to anyone around Derringer and Lucia they were madly in love with each other.

Later that day they had dinner with Ramsey and Chloe and enjoyed the time they spent with the couple immensely. Over dinner Ramsey provided tidbits about sheep ranching and how he'd made the decision to move from being a businessman to operating a sheep ranch.

The sun was going down when she and Jason mounted their horses to return to her ranch. It had been a full day of activities and she had learned a lot about both the horse training business and sheep ranching.

She glanced over at Jason. He hadn't said a whole lot since they'd left his brother's ranch and she couldn't help wondering what he was thinking. She also couldn't help wondering if he intended to sleep in his truck again tonight.

"I feel like a freeloader today," she said to break the silence between them.

He glanced over at her. "Why?"

"Your family fed me breakfast, lunch and dinner today."

He smiled. "They like you."

"And I like them."

She truly did. One of the benefits of accepting Jason's proposal would be his family. But what would happen after the year was up and she'd gotten attached to them? Considered herself part of the family?

They had cleared his land and were riding on her property when up ahead in the distance they saw what appeared to be a huge fiery red ball filled with smoke. They both realized at the same time what it was.

Fire.

And it was coming from the direction of her ranch.

Seven

Bella stood in what used to be the middle of her living room, glanced around and fought the tears stinging her eyes. More than half of her home was gone, destroyed by the fire. And according to the fire marshal it had been deliberately set. If it hadn't been for the quick thinking of her men who begun using water hoses to douse the flames, the entire ranch house would have gone up in smoke.

Her heart felt heavy. Oppressed. Broken. All she'd wanted when she had left Savannah was to start a new life here. But it seemed that was not going to happen. Someone wanted her gone. Who wanted her land that much?

She felt a touch to her arm and without looking up she knew it was Jason. Her body would recognize his touch anywhere. He had been by her side the entire time and watched as portions of her house went up in flames. And he had held her when she couldn't watch any longer and buried her face in his chest and clung to him. At that moment he had become the one thing that was unshakable in a world that was falling down all around her; intentionally being destroyed by someone who was determined to steal her happiness and joy. And he had held her and whispered over and over that everything was going to be all right. And she had tried to believe him and had managed to draw strength from him.

His family had arrived and had given their support as well and had let the authorities know they wanted answers and wanted the person or persons responsible brought to justice. Already they were talking about helping her rebuild and like Jason had done, assured her that everything would be all right.

Sheriff Harper had questioned her, making inquiries similar to the ones Pete had yesterday when the rock had been thrown through her living room window. Did she know of anyone who wanted her out of Denver? Whoever was responsible was determined to get their message through to her loud and clear.

"Bella?"

She glanced up and met Jason's gaze. "Yes?"

"Come on, let's go. There's nothing more we can do here tonight."

She shuddered miserably and the lungs holding back her sob constricted. "Go? Go where, Jason? Look around you. I no longer have a home."

She couldn't stop the single tear that fell from her eyes. Instead of responding to what she'd said Jason brushed the tear away with the pad of his thumb before entwining his fingers in hers. He then led her away toward the barn for a moment of privacy. It was then that he turned her to face him, sweeping the curls back from her face. He fixed her with a gaze that stirred everything inside of her.

"As long as I have a home, Bella, you do, too."

He then drew in a deep breath. "Don't let whoever did this win. This is land that your grandfather gave you and you have every right to be here if that's what you want. Don't let anyone run you off your land," Jason said in a husky whisper.

She heard his words, she felt his plea, but like she'd told him, she no longer had a home now. She didn't want to depend on others, become their charity case. "But what can I do, Jason? It takes money to rebuild and thanks to my parents, my trust fund is on hold." She paused and then with sagging shoulders added, "I don't have anything now. The ranch was insured, but it will take time to rebuild."

"You have me, Bella. My proposal still stands and now more than ever you should consider taking it. A marriage between us means that we'll both get what we want and will show the person who did this that you aren't going anywhere. It will show them they didn't win after all and sooner or later they will get caught. And even if it happens to be a member of your family, I'm going to make sure they pay for doing this."

Jason lowered his gaze to the ground for a moment and then returned it to her. "I am worse than mad right now, Bella, I'm so full of rage I could actually hurt someone for doing this to you. Whoever is behind this probably thought you were inside the house. What if you had been? What if you hadn't spent the day with me?"

Bella took a deep breath. Those were more "what ifs" she didn't want to think about or consider. The only thing she wanted to think about right now was the proposal; the one Jason had offered and still wanted her to take. And she decided at that very moment that she would.

She would take her chances on what might or might not happen within that year. She would be the best wife possible and hopefully in a year's time even if he wanted a divorce they could still be friends.

"So what about it, Bella? Will you show whoever did this today that you are a fighter and not a quitter and that you will keep what's yours? Will you marry me so we can do that together?"

She held his gaze, exhaled deeply. "Yes, I'll marry you, Jason."

She thought the smile that touched his lips was priceless and she had to inwardly remind herself he wasn't happy because he was marrying her but because marrying her meant he would co-own her land and get full possession of Hercules. And in marrying him she would get her trust fund back and send a message to whomever was behind the threats to her that they were wasting their time and she wasn't going anywhere.

He leaned down, brushed a kiss across her lips and tightened his hold on her hand. "Come on. Let's go tell the family our good news."

If Jason's brothers and cousins were surprised by their announcement they didn't let on. Probably because they were too busy congratulating them and then making wedding plans.

She and Jason had decided the true nature of their marriage was between them. They planned to keep it that way. The Westmorelands didn't so much as bat an eye when Jason further announced they would be getting married as soon as possible. Tomorrow in fact. He assured everyone they could plan a huge reception for later.

Bella decided to contact her parents *after* the wedding tomorrow. A judge who was a friend of the Westmorelands was given a call and he immediately agreed to perform the civil ceremony in his chambers around three in the afternoon. Dillon and Ramsey suggested the family celebrate the nuptials by joining them for dinner after the ceremony at a restaurant downtown.

The honeymoon would come later. For now they would spend the night at a hotel downtown. With so many things to do to prepare for tomorrow, Bella was able to put the fire behind her and she actually looked forward to her wedding day. She was also able to put out of her mind the reason they were marrying in the first place. Dillon and Pam invited her to spend the night in their home, and she accepted their invitation.

"Come walk me out to my truck," Jason whispered, taking her hand in his.

"All right."

When they got to where his truck was parked, he placed her against it and leaned over and kissed her in a deep, drugging kiss. When he released her lips he whispered, "You can come home with me tonight, you know."

Yes, she knew but then she also knew if she did so, they would consummate a wedding that was yet to take place. She wanted to do things in the right order. The way she'd always dreamed of doing them when she read all those romance novels.

"Yes, I know but I'll be fine staying with Dillon and Pam tonight. Tomorrow will be here before you know it." She then paused and looked up at him, searched his gaze. "And you think we're doing the right thing, Jason?"

He smiled, nodding. "Yes, I'm positive. After the ceremony we'll contact your parents and provide their attorney with whatever documentation needed to kick your trust fund back in gear. And I'm sure word will get around soon enough for whoever has been making those threats to hear Bella Bostwick Westmoreland is here to stay."

Bella Bostwick Westmoreland. She liked the sound of it already but deep down she knew she couldn't get attached to it. She stared into his eyes and hoped he wouldn't wake up one morning and think he'd made a mistake and the proposal hadn't been worth it.

"Everything will work out for the best, Bella. You'll see." He then pulled her into his arms and kissed her again.

"I now pronounce you man and wife. Jason, you may kiss your bride."

Jason didn't waste any time pulling Bella into his arms and devouring her mouth the way he'd gotten accustomed to doing.

He had expected a small audience but every Westmoreland living in Denver was there, except Micah, his brother who was a year older and an epidemiologist with the federal government, as well as his brothers Canyon and Stern who were away attending law school. And of course he missed his cousin Gemma who was living with her husband in Australia, and his younger brother Bane who was in the navy. Jason also missed the twins, Aiden and Adrian. They were away at college.

When he finally released Bella's mouth, cheers went

up and he glanced at Bella and knew at that moment just how much he loved her. He would prove the depth of his love over the rest of their lives. He knew she assumed after the first year either of them could file for divorce, but he didn't intend for that to happen. Ever. There would be no divorce.

He glanced down at the ring he'd placed on her finger. He had picked her up at eight that morning, taken her into town for breakfast and from there a whirlwind of activities had begun with a visit to the jeweler. Then to the courthouse to file the necessary papers so they could marry on time. Luckily there was no waiting period in Colorado and he was grateful for that.

"Hey, Jason and Bella. Are the two of you ready for dinner?" Dillon asked, smiling.

Jason smiled back. "Yes, we are." He took Bella's hand in his, felt the sensations touching her elicited and knew that, personally, he was ready for something else, as well.

Bella cast a quick glance over at Jason as they stepped on the elevator that would take them up to their hotel room in the tower—the honeymoon suite—compliments of the entire Westmoreland family. She realized she hadn't just married the man but had also inherited his entire family. For someone who'd never had an extended family before, she could only be elated.

Dinner with everyone had been wonderful and Jason's brothers and cousins had stood to offer toasts to what everyone saw as a long marriage. There hadn't been anything in Jason's expression indicating they were way off base in that assumption or that it was wishful thinking on their parts.

All of the Westmoreland ladies had given her hugs

and welcomed her to the family. The men had hugged her, as well, and she could tell they were genuinely happy for her and Jason.

And now they were on the elevator that would carry them to the floor where their room was located. They would be spending the night, sleeping under the same roof and sharing the same bed. They hadn't discussed such a thing happening, but she knew it was an unspoken understanding between them.

Jason had become quiet and she wondered if he'd already regretted making the proposal. The thought that he had sent her into a panic mode, made her heart begin to break a piece at a time. Then without warning, she felt his hand touch her arm and when she glanced over at him he smiled and reached for her and pulled her closer to his side, as if refusing to let her stand anywhere by herself…without him. It was as if he was letting her know she would never ever be alone again.

She knew a part of her was probably rationalizing things the way she wished they were, the way she wanted them to be but not necessarily how they really were. But if she had to fantasize then she would do that. If she had to pretend they had a real marriage for the next year then she would do that, too. However, a part of her would never lose sight of the real reason she was here. A part of her would always be prepared for the inevitable.

"You were a beautiful bride, Bella."

"Thank you." Warmth spread through her in knowing that he'd thought so because she had tried so hard to be. She had been determined to make some part of today resemble a real wedding—even if it was a civil one in the judge's chambers. The ladies in the family had insisted that she be turned over to them after securing a license at the Denver County Court House and had promised Jason she would be on time for her wedding.

It had taken less than an hour to obtain the marriage license and Lucia had been there to pick her up afterward. Bella had been whisked away for a day of beauty and to visit a very exclusive bridal shop to pick up the perfect dress for her wedding. Since time was of the essence, everything had been arranged beforehand. When they had delivered her back to Jason five hours later, the moment she'd joined him in the judge's chambers his smile had let her know he thought her time away from him had been well worth it. She would forever be grateful to her new in-laws and a part of her knew that Pam, Chloe, Megan, Lucia and Bailey would also be friends she could count on for life.

"You look good yourself," she said softly.

She thought that was an understatement. She had seen him in a suit the night at the charity ball. He had taken her breath away then and was taking it away now. Tall, dark and handsome, he was the epitome of every woman's fantasy and dream. And for at least one full year, he would be hers.

The elevator stopped on their floor and tightening his hand on hers, they stepped out. Her breath caught when the elevator doors whooshed closed behind them and they began walking toward room 4501. She knew once they reached those doors and she stepped inside there would be no turning back.

They silently strolled side by side holding hands. Everything about the Four Seasons Hotel spoke of its elegance and the decorative colors all around were vibrant and vivid.

Jason released her hand when they reached their room to pull the passkey from the pocket of his suit jacket.

Once he opened the door he extended his hand to her and she took it, felt the sensations flowing between them. She gasped when she was suddenly swept off her feet and into his arms and carried over the threshold into the honeymoon suite.

Jason kicked the door closed with his foot before placing Bella on her feet. And then he just stood there and looked at her, allowing his gaze to roam all over her. What he'd told her earlier was true. She was a beautiful bride.

And she was his.

Absolutely and positively his.

Her tea-length dress was ivory in color and made of silk chiffon and fitted at her small waist with a rose in the center. It was a perfect match for the ivory satin rose-heeled shoes on her feet. White roses were her favorite flower and she'd used them as the theme in their wedding. Even her wedding bouquet had consisted of white roses.

His chest expanded with so much love for her, love she didn't know about yet. He had a year to win her over and intended to spend the next twelve months doing just that. But now, he needed for her to know just how much she was desired.

He lowered his head and kissed her, letting his tongue tangle with hers, reacquainting himself with the taste of her, a taste he had not forgotten and had so desperately craved since the last time. He kissed her deeply, not allowing any part of her mouth to go untouched. And she returned the kiss with a hunger that matched his own and he was mesmerized by how she was making him feel.

He tightened his hold on her, molding his body to

hers, and was certain she could feel the hot ridge of his erection pressing against her. It was throbbing something awful with a need for her that was monumental. He had wanted her for a long time…ever since he'd seen her that night at the ball, and his desire for her hadn't diminished any since. If anything, it had only increased to a level that even now he could feel his gut tighten in desire. Taking her hands he deliberately began slowly lifting her dress up toward her waist.

"Wrap your legs around me, Bella," he whispered and assisted by lifting her hips when she wrapped her legs around him to walk her toward the bedroom. It was a huge suite and he was determined that later, after they took care of business in the bedroom, they would check out all the amenities the suite had to offer; especially the large Jacuzzi bathtub. Already he saw the beauty of downtown Denver from their hotel room window. But downtown Denver was the last thing on his mind right now. Making love to his wife was.

His wife.

He began kissing her again, deeper and longer, loving the way her tongue mated with his over and over again. He placed her on the bed while reaching behind her to unfasten her dress and slide it from her body. It was then that he took a step back and thought he was dreaming. No fantasy could top what he was seeing now.

She was wearing a white lace bra and matching panties. On any other woman such a color would come across as ultrainnocence, but on Bella it became the epitome of sexual desire.

He needed to completely undress her and did so while thinking of everything he wanted to do to her. When she was on her knees in the middle of the bed naked, he could tell from her expression that this was the first time a man had seen her body and the thought sent shivers through him as his gaze roamed over her in male appreciation. A shudder of primal pride flowed through him and he could only stand there and take her all in.

An erection that was already hard got even harder when he looked at her chest, an area he had yet to taste. Her twin globes were firm. His tongue tingled at the thought of being wrapped around those nipples.

No longer able to resist temptation, he moved toward the bed and placed a knee on it and immediately leaned in to capture a nipple in his mouth. His tongue latched on the hard nub and began playing all kinds of games with it. Games she seemed to enjoy if the way she was pushing her breasts deeper into his mouth was anything to go by.

He heard her moan as he continued to torture her nipples, with quick nips followed by sucking motions and when he reached down to let his hands test her to see how ready she was, he found she was definitely ready for him. Pulling back he eased from the bed to remove his clothes as she watched.

"I'm not on the Pill, Jason."

He glanced over at her. "You're not?"

"No."

And evidently thinking she needed to explain further she said, "I haven't been sexually active with anyone."

"Since?"

"Never."

A part of him wasn't surprised. In fact he had suspected as much. He'd known no other man had performed oral sex on her but hadn't been sure of the depth of any other sexual experience. "Any reason you hadn't?"

She met his gaze and held it. "I've been waiting for you."

He drew in a sharp breath and wondered if she knew what she'd just insinuated and figured she hadn't. Maybe she hadn't insinuated anything and it was just wishful thinking on his part. He loved her and would give just about anything for her to love him in return. And until she said the words, he wouldn't assume anything.

"Then your wait is over, sweetheart," he said, sliding on a condom over the thickness of his erection while she looked on. And from the fascinated expression on her face he could tell what she was seeing was another first for her.

When he completed that task he moved to the bed and toward her. "You are so beautifully built, Jason," she said softly, and as if she needed to test her ability to arouse him, she leaned up and flicked out her tongue, licking one of the hardened nubs on his breast like he'd done earlier to her.

He drew in a sharp intake of breath. "You're a quick learner," he said huskily.

"Is that good or bad?"

He smiled at her. "For us it will always be good."

Since this would be her first time he wanted her more than ready and knew of one way to do it. He eased her down on the bed and decided to lick her into an orgasm. Starting at her mouth, he slowly moved downward to her chin, trekked down her neck to her breasts. By the time he'd made it past her midriff to her flat tummy she was writhing under his mouth but he didn't mind. That was a telltale sign of how she was feeling.

"Open your legs, baby," he whispered. The moment she did so he dipped his head to ease his tongue between the folds of her femininity. He recalled doing this to her the last time and knew just what spots would make her moan deep in her throat. Tonight he wanted to do better than that. He wanted to make her scream.

Over and over again he licked her to the edge of an orgasm then withdrew his tongue and began torturing her all over again. She sobbed his name, moaned and groaned. And then, when she was on the verge of an explosion he shifted upward and placed his body over hers.

When he guided his erection in place, he held her gaze and lowered his body to join with hers, uniting them as one. She was tight and he kept a level of control as he eased inside her, feeling how firm a hold her clenched muscles had on him. He didn't want to hurt her and moved inch by slow inch inside her. When he had finally reached the hilt, he closed his eyes but didn't move. He needed to be still for a moment and grasp the significance of what was taking place. He was making love to his wife and she was a wife he loved more than life.

He slowly opened his eyes and met hers and saw she had been watching…waiting and needing him to finish what he'd started. So he did. He began moving slowly, with an extremely low amount of pressure as he began moving in and out of her. When she arched her back, he increased the pressure and the rhythm.

The sounds she began making sent him spiraling and let him know she was loving it. The more she moaned, the more she got. Several times he'd gone so deep inside her he knew he had touched her womb and the thought that he had done so made him crave her that much more.

She released a number of shuddering breaths as he continued to thrust, claiming her as his while she claimed him as hers. And then she threw her head back and screamed out his name.

That's when he came, filling her while groaning thickly as an orgasm overtook them both. The spasms that rammed through his body were so powerful he had to force himself to breathe. He bucked against her several times as he continued to ride her through the force of his release.

He inhaled the scent of their lovemaking before leaning down to capture her mouth, and knew at that moment the night for them was just beginning.

Sometime during the night Jason woke up from the feel of Bella's mouth on him. Immediately his erection began to swell.

"Oh." She pulled her mouth away and looked up at him with a blush on her face. "I thought you were asleep."

His lips curved into a smile. "I was but there are some things a man can't sleep through. What are you doing down there?"

She raised her head to meet his gaze. "Tasting you the way you tasted me," she said softly.

"You didn't have to wait until I was asleep, you know," he said, feeling himself get even harder. Although he was no longer inside her mouth, it was still close. Right there. And the heat of her breath was way too close.

"I know, but you were asleep and I thought I would practice first. I didn't want to embarrass myself while you were awake and get it wrong," she said, blushing even more.

He chuckled, thinking her blush was priceless. "Baby, this is one of those things a woman can never get wrong."

"Do you want me to stop?"

"What do you think?"

She smiled up at him shyly. Wickedly. Wantonly. "I think you don't. Just remember this is a practice session."

She then leaned closer and slid him back into her mouth. He groaned deep in his throat when she began making love to him this way. Earlier that night he had licked her into an orgasm and now she was licking him to insanity. He made a low sound in the back of his throat when she began pulling everything out of him with her mouth. If this was a practice session she would kill him when it came to the real thing.

"Bella!"

He quickly reached down and pulled her up to him and flipped her onto her back. He moved on top of her and pushed inside of her, realizing too late when he felt himself explode that he wasn't wearing a condom. The thought that he could be making her pregnant jutted an even bigger release from his body into hers.

His entire body quivered from the magnitude of the powerful thrusts that kept coming, thrusts he wasn't able to stop. The more she gave, the more he wanted and when her hips arched off the bed, he drove in deeper and came again.

"Jason!"

She was following him to sweet oblivion and his heart began hammering at the realization that this was lovemaking as naked as it could get, and he clung to it, clung to her. A low, shivering moan escaped his lips and when her thighs began to tremor, he felt the vibration to the core.

Moments later he collapsed on top of her, moaned her name as his manhood buried inside of her continued to throb, cling to her flesh as her inner muscles wouldn't release their hold.

What they'd just shared as well as all the other times they'd made love tonight was so unbearably pleasurable he couldn't think straight. The thought of what she'd been doing when he had awakened sent sensuous chills down his body.

He opened his mouth to speak but immediately closed it when he saw she had drifted off to sleep. She made such an erotic picture lying there with her eyes closed, soft dark curls framing her face and the sexiest lips he'd ever had the pleasure of kissing slightly parted.

He continued to look at her, thinking he would let her get some rest now. Later he intended to wake her up the same way she'd woken him.

Eight

The following morning after they'd enjoyed breakfast in bed, Bella figured now was just as good a time as any to let her parents know she was a married woman.

She picked up her cell phone and then glanced over at Jason and smiled. That smile gave her the inner strength for the confrontation she knew was coming. The thought of her outwitting them by marrying—and someone from Denver—would definitely throw her parents into a tizzy. She could just imagine what they would try to do. But just as Jason had said, they could try but wouldn't succeed. She and Jason were as married as married could get and there was nothing her parents could do about it.

Taking a deep breath she punched in their number and when the housekeeper answered she was put on hold, waiting for her father to pick up the line.

"Elizabeth. I hope you're calling to say you've come

to your senses and have purchased a one-way plane ticket back home."

She frowned. He didn't even take the time to ask how she was doing. Although she figured her parents had nothing to do with those two incidents this week, she decided to ask anyway. "Tell me something, Dad. Did you and Mom think using scare tactics to get me to return to Savannah would work?"

"What are you talking about?"

"Three days ago someone threw a rock through my living room window with a threatening note for me to leave town, and two days ago someone torched my house. Luckily I wasn't there at the time."

"Someone set Dad's house on fire?"

She'd heard the shock in his voice and she heard something else, too. Empathy. This was the first time she'd heard him refer to Herman as "Dad."

"Yes."

"I didn't have anything to do with that, Elizabeth. Your mother and I would never put you in danger like that. What kind of parents do you think we are?"

"Controlling. But I didn't call to exchange words, Dad. I'm just calling for you and Mother to share my good news. I got married yesterday."

"What!"

"That's right. I got married to a wonderful man by the name of Jason Westmoreland."

"Westmoreland?"

"Yes."

"I went to schools with some Westmorelands. Their land was connected to ours."

"Probably his parents. They're deceased now."

"Sorry to hear that, but I hope you know why he married you. He wants that land. But don't worry about it, dear. It can easily be remedied once you file for an annulment."

She shook her head. Her parents just didn't get it. "Jason didn't force me to marry him, Dad. I married him of my own free will."

"Listen, Elizabeth, you haven't been living out there even a full month. You don't know this guy. I will not allow you to marry him."

"Dad, I am already married to him and I plan to send your attorney a copy of our marriage license so the hold on my trust fund will be lifted."

"You think you're smart, Elizabeth. I know what you're doing and I won't allow it. You don't love him and he can't love you."

"Sounds pretty much like the same setup you and Mom have got going. The same kind of marriage you wanted me to enter with Hugh. So what's the problem? I don't see where there is one and I refuse to discuss the matter with you any longer. Goodbye, Dad. Give Mom my best." She then clicked off the phone.

"I take it the news of our marriage didn't go over well with your father."

She glanced over at Jason who was lying beside her and smiled faintly. "Did you really expect that it would?"

"No and it really doesn't matter. They'll just have to get over it."

She snuggled closer to him. That was one of the things she liked about Jason. He was his own man. "What time do we have to check out of here?"

"By noon. And then we'll be on our way to Jason's Place."

She had to restrain the happiness she felt upon knowing they would be going to his home where she would live for at least the next twelve months. "Are there any do's and don'ts that I need to know about?"

He lifted a brow. "Do's and don'ts?"

"Yes. My time at your home is limited. I don't want to jeopardize my welcome." She could have sworn she'd seen something flash in his eyes but couldn't be certain.

"You'd never jeopardize your welcome and no, there are no do's and don'ts that will apply to you, unless..."

Now it was her turn to raise a brow. "Unless what?"

"You take a notion to paint my bedroom pink or something."

She couldn't help bursting out in laughter. She calmed down enough to ask, "What about yellow? Will that do?"

"Not one of my favorite colors but I guess it will work."

She smiled as she snuggled even closer to him. She was looking forward to living under the same roof with Jason.

"Bella?"

She glanced up. "Yes?"

"The last time we made love, I didn't use a condom."

She'd been aware of it but hadn't expected him to talk about it. "Yes, I know."

"It wasn't intentional."

"I know that, too," she said softly. There was no reason he would want to get her pregnant. That would only throw a monkey wrench in their agreement.

They didn't say anything for a long moment and then he asked, "Do you like children?"

She wondered why he was asking such a thing. Surely

he had seen her interactions with Susan and Denver enough to know that she did. "Yes, I like children."

"Do you think you'd want any of your own one day?"

Was he asking because he was worried that she would use that as a trap to stay with him beyond the one year? But he'd asked and she needed to be honest. "Yes, I'd love children, although I haven't had the best of childhoods. Don't get me wrong, my parents weren't monsters or anything like that but they just weren't affectionate...at least not like your family."

She paused for a moment. "I love my parents, Jason, although I doubt my relationship with them will ever be what I've always wished for. They aren't that kind of people. Displaying affection isn't one of their strong points. If I become a mother I want to do just the opposite. There will never be a day my child will not know he or she is loved." She hadn't meant to say all of that and now she couldn't help wondering if doing so would ruin things between them.

"I think you would make a wonderful mother."

His words touched her. "Thank you for saying that."

"You're welcome, and I meant it."

She drew in a deep breath, wondering how he could be certain of such a thing. She continued to stare at him for a long moment. He would be a gift to any woman and he had sacrificed himself to marry her—just because he'd wanted her land and Hercules. When she thought about it she found it pitiful that it had taken that to make him want to join his life to hers.

He lifted her hand and looked at the ring he'd placed there. She looked at it, too. It was beautiful. More than she'd expected and everyone had oohed and aahed over it.

"You're wearing my ring," he said softly.

The sound of his deep, husky voice made her tummy tingle and a heated sensation spread all through her. "Yes, I'm wearing your ring. It's beautiful. Thank you."

Then she lifted his hand. Saw the gold band brilliantly shining in the sunlight. "And you're wearing mine."

And then she found herself being kissed by him and she knew that no matter how their marriage might end up, right now it was off to a great beginning.

For the second time in two days Jason carried the woman he loved over the threshold. This time he walked into his house. "Welcome to Jason's Place, sweetheart," he said, placing her on her feet.

Bella glanced around. This was the first time she'd been inside Jason's home. She'd seen it a few times from a distance and thought the two-story dwelling flanked by a number of flowering trees was simply beautiful. On the drive from town he'd given her a little history of his home. It had taken an entire year to build and he had built it himself, with help from all the other Westmorelands. And with all the pride she'd heard when he spoke of it, she knew he loved his home. She could see why. The design was magnificent. The decorating—which had been done by his cousin Gemma—was breathtaking and perfect for the single man he'd been.

Jason's eyes never left Bella's as he studied her reaction to being in his home. As far as he was concerned, she would be a permanent fixture. His heart would beat when hers did. His breath was released the same time hers was. He had shared something with her he had never done with any woman—the essence of himself. For the first time in his life he had made love to a woman without wearing a condom. It had felt wonderful being skin to skin, flesh to flesh with her—but only with her. The wife he adored and intended to keep forever.

He knew he had a job to do where she was concerned and it would be one that would give him the greatest of pleasure and satisfaction. Her pain was his pain, her happiness was his. Their lives were now entwined and all because of the proposal he'd offered and she'd taken.

Without thought he turned her in his arms and lowered his head to kiss her, needing the feel of his mouth on hers, her body pressed against his. The kiss was long, deep and the most satisfying experience he could imagine. But then, he'd had nothing but satisfying experiences with her. And he planned on having plenty more.

"Aren't you going to work today?" Bella asked Jason the following day over breakfast. She was learning her way around his spacious kitchen and loved doing it. They had stayed inside yesterday after he'd brought her here. He had kept her mostly in the bedroom, saying their honeymoon was still ongoing. And she had been not one to argue considering the glow she figured had to be on her face. Jason was the most ardent and generous of lovers.

Her mother had called last night trying to convince her she'd made a mistake and that she and her father would be flying into Denver in a few days to talk some sense into her. Bella had told her mother she didn't think coming to Denver was a good idea, but of course Melissa Bostwick wouldn't listen.

When Bella had told Jason about the latest developments—namely her parents' planned trip to Denver—he'd merely shrugged and told her not to worry about it. That was easy for him to say. He'd never met her parents.

"No, I'm not going to work today. I'm still on my honeymoon," Jason said, breaking into her thoughts. "You tell me what you want to do today and we'll do it."

She turned away from the stove where she'd prepared something simple like French toast. "You want to spend more time with me?"

He chuckled. "Of course I do. You sound surprised."

She was. She figured as much time as they'd spent in the bedroom he would have tired of her by now. She was about to open her mouth when his house phone rang. He smiled over at her. "Excuse me for a minute while I get that."

Bella figured the caller was one of his relatives. She turned back to the stove to turn it off. She couldn't help but smile at the thought that he wanted to spend more time with her.

A few moments later Jason hung up the phone. "That was Sheriff Harper."

She turned back around to him. "Has he found out anything?"

"Yes, they've made some arrests."

A lump formed in her throat. She crossed the floor to sit down at the table, thinking she didn't want to be standing for this. "Who did it?"

He came to sit across from her. "Your uncle Kenneth's twin grandsons."

Bella's hand flew to her chest. "But they're only fourteen years old."

"Yes, but the footprints outside your window and the fingerprints on the rock matched theirs. Not to mention that the kerosene can they used to start the fire at your ranch belonged to their parents."

Bella didn't say anything. She just continued to stare at him.

"Evidently they heard their grandfather's grumblings about you and figured they were doing him a favor by scaring you away," Jason said.

"What will happen to them?" she asked quietly.

"Right now they're in police custody. A judge will decide tomorrow if they will be released into the custody of their parents until a court date is set. If they are found guilty, and chances are they will be since the evidence against them is so strong, they will serve time in a detention center for youth for about one or two years, maybe longer depending on any prior arrests."

Jason's face hardened. "Personally, it wouldn't bother me in the least if they locked them up and threw away the key. I'm sure Kenneth is fit to be tied, though. He thinks the world of those two."

Bella shook her head sadly. "I feel so badly about this."

A deep scowl covered Jason's face. "Why do you feel badly? You're the victim and they broke the law."

She could tell by the sound of his voice that he was still upset. "But they're just kids. I need to call Uncle Kenneth."

"Why? As far as I'm concerned this is all his fault for spouting off at the mouth around them about you."

A part of Bella knew what Jason said was true and could even accept he had a right to be angry, but still, the thought that she was responsible for the disruption of so many lives was getting to her. Had she made a mistake in moving to Denver after all?

"Don't even think it, Bella."

She glanced across the table at Jason. "What?"

"I know what's going through your mind, sweetheart. I can see it all over your face and you want to blame yourself for what happened but it's not your fault."

"Isn't it?"

"No. You can't hold yourself responsible for the actions of others. What if you had been standing near the window the day that rock came flying through, or worse yet, what if you'd been home the day they set fire to the house? If I sound mad it's because I still am. And I'm going to stay mad until justice is served."

He paused a moment and then said, "I don't want to talk about Kenneth or his grandsons any longer. Come on, let's get dressed and go riding."

When they returned from riding and Bella checked her cell phone, she had received a call from her parents saying that they had changed their minds and would not be coming to Denver after all. She couldn't help wondering why, but she figured the best thing to do was count her blessings and be happy about their change in plans.

Jason was outside putting the horses away and she decided to take a shower and change into something relaxing. So far, other than the sheriff, no one else had called. She figured Jason's family was treating them as honeymooners and giving them their privacy.

When her cell phone rang, she didn't recognize the caller but figured it might be one of her parents calling from another number. "Yes?"

"This is all your fault, Bella."

She froze upon hearing her uncle's voice. He was angry. "My grandsons might be going to some youth detention center for a couple of years because of you."

Bella drew in a deep breath and remembered the conversation she and Jason had had earlier that day. "You should not have talked badly about me in front of them."

"Are you saying it's my fault?"

"Yes, Uncle Kenneth, that's exactly what I'm saying. You have no one else to blame but yourself."

"Why you… How dare you speak to me that way. You think you're something now that you're married to a Westmoreland. Well, you'll see what a mistake you made. All Jason Westmoreland wanted was your land and that horse. He doesn't care anything about you. I told you I knew someone who wanted to buy your land."

"And I've always told you my land isn't for sale."

"If you don't think Westmoreland plans to weasel it from you then you're crazy. Just mark my word. You mean nothing to him. All he wants is that land. He is nothing but a controller and a manipulator."

Her uncle then hung up the phone on her.

Bella tried not to let her uncle's words get to her. No one knew the details of their marriage so her uncle had no idea that she was well aware that Jason wanted her land and horse. For what other reason would he have presented her with that proposal? She wasn't the crazy person her uncle evidently assumed she was. She was operating with more than a full deck and was also well aware Jason didn't love her.

She glanced up when Jason walked through the back door. He smiled when he saw her. "I thought you were going to take a shower."

"I was, but I got a phone call."

"Oh, from who?"

She knew now was not the time to tell him about her uncle's call—especially after all he'd said earlier. So she decided to take that time to tell him about her parents' decision.

"Dad and Mom called. They aren't coming after all."

"What changed their minds?" he asked, taking a seat on the sofa.

"Not sure. They didn't say."

He caught her wrist and pulled her down on the sofa beside him. "Well, I have a lot to say, none of it nice. But the main thing is they've decided not to come and I think it's a good move on their part because I don't want anyone to upset you."

"No one will," she said softly. "I'm fine."

"And I want to make sure you stay that way," he said and pulled her closer into his arms.

She was quiet as her head lay rested against his chest and could actually hear his heart pounding. She wondered if he could hear the pounding of her heart. She still found it strange how attracted they were to each other. Getting married hadn't lessened that any.

She lifted her head to look up at him and saw the intense look that was there in his eyes. It was a look that was so intimate it sent a rush of heat sprinting all through her.

And when he began easing his mouth toward hers, all thoughts left her mind except for one, and that was how much he could make her feel loved even when he was pretending. The moment their lips touched she refused to believe her uncle Kenneth's claim that he was controlling.

Instead she concentrated on how he was making her feel with the way his mouth was mating with hers. And she knew this kiss was just the beginning.

Nine

During the next few weeks Bella settled into what she considered a comfortable routine. She'd never thought being married would be such a wonderful experience and could only thank Jason for making the transition easy for her.

They shared a bed and made passionate love each night. Then in the morning they would get up early and while he sat at the table drinking coffee she would enjoy a cup of tea while he told her about what horses he would be training that day.

While he was away she usually kept busy by reading her grandfather's journals, which had been upstairs in her bedroom and so were spared by the fire. Because she'd been heavily involved with a lot of charity work while living in Savannah, she'd already volunteered a lot of her time at the children's hospital and the Westmoreland Foundation.

Hercules was now in Jason's stalls and Jason was working with the insurance company on the repairs of her ranch. He had arranged for all the men who'd worked with her before the fire to be hired on with his horse training business.

Although she appreciated him stepping in and taking charge of her affairs the way he'd done, she hadn't been able to put her uncle Kenneth's warning out of her mind. She knew it was ludicrous to worry about Jason's motivation because he had been honest with her from the beginning and she knew why he'd made the proposal for their marriage. She was well aware that he didn't love her and that he was only married to her for the land and Hercules. But now that he had both was it just a matter of time for him before he tried to get rid of her?

She would be the first to admit he never acted as if he was getting tired of her and still treated her as if he enjoyed having her around. In the afternoons when he returned home for work, the first thing he did after placing his Stetson on the hat rack was to seek her out. Usually he didn't have far to look because she would be right there, close by. Anticipating his return home always put her near the door when he entered the house.

Bella couldn't help noticing that over the last couple of days she had begun getting a little antsy where Jason was concerned because she was uncertain as to her future with him. And to make matters even worse she was late, which was a good sign she might be pregnant. She hadn't told him of her suspicions because she wasn't sure how he would take the news.

If she were pregnant, the baby would be born within the first year of their marriage. Would he still want a divorce even if she was the mother of his child or would he want to keep her around for that same reason; because he felt obligated to do so? But an even more important question was, did he even want to become a father? He had questioned her feelings on motherhood but she'd never questioned his. She could tell from his interactions with Susan and Denver that he liked kids, but that didn't necessarily mean he wanted any of his own.

Bella knew she should tell him about the possibility she could be pregnant and discuss her concerns with him now, but each time she was presented with the opportunity to do so, she would get cold feet.

She walked into an empty room he'd converted into an office and sat down at the desk to glance out the window. She would finally admit that another reason she was antsy was that she knew without a shadow of doubt that she had fallen in love with Jason and could certainly understand how such a thing had happened. She could understand it, but would he? He'd never asked for her love, just her land and horse.

She heard the sound of a vehicle door closing and stood from the desk, went to the window and looked down. It was Jason. He glanced up and saw her and a smile touched the corners of his mouth. Instantly she felt the buds of her nipples harden against her blouse. A flush of desire rushed through her and she knew at that moment her panties had gotten wet. The man could turn her on with a single look. He was home earlier than usual. Three hours earlier.

Now that he was here a lot of ideas flowed in her mind on how they could use those extra hours. What she wanted to do first was to take him into her mouth, something she discovered she enjoyed doing. And then he could return the favor by putting that tongue of his to work between her legs. She shuddered at the thought and figured her hormones were on the attack; otherwise, she wouldn't be thinking such scandalous things. They were definitely not things a Miss Prim and Proper lady would think.

He broke eye contact with her to walk up the steps to come into the house and she rushed out of the office to stand at the top of the stairs. She glanced down the moment he opened the door. Jason's dark gaze latched on her and immediately her breath was snatched from her lungs. As she watched, he locked the door behind him and slowly began removing the clothes from his body, first tossing his hat on the rack and then unbuttoning his shirt.

She felt hot as she watched him and he didn't stop. He had completely removed his shirt and she couldn't help admiring the broad shoulders and sinewy muscular thighs in jeans. The masculine sight had blood rushing fast and furious through her veins.

"I'm coming up," he said in a deep, husky voice.

She slowly began backing up when he started moving up the stairs with a look in his eyes that was as predatory as anything she'd ever seen. And there was a deep, intense hunger in his gaze that had her heart hammering like crazy in her chest.

When he cleared the top stair and stepped onto the landing, she breathed in deeply, taking in his scent, while thinking that no man had a right to smell so good, look so utterly male and be so damn hot in a way that would overwhelm any woman's senses.

At least no man but Jason Westmoreland.

"Take off your clothes, Bella," he said in a deep, throaty voice.

She then asked what some would probably think was a dumb question. "Why?"

He moved slowly toward her and it was as if her feet were glued to the spot and she couldn't move. And when he came to a stop in front of her, she tilted back her head to look up at him, saw the hunger in his dark brown gaze. The intensity of that look sent a shudder through her.

He reached out and cupped her face in the palms of his hands and lowered his head slightly to whisper, "I came home early because I need to make love to you. And I need to do it now."

And then he captured her mouth with his, kissing her with the same intensity and hunger she'd seen in his eyes. She returned his kiss, not understanding why he needed to make love to her and why now. But she knew she would give him whatever he wanted and whatever way he wanted it.

He was ravishing her mouth, making her moan deep in her throat. His kiss seemed to be making a statement and staking a claim all at the same time. She couldn't do anything but take whatever he was giving, and she did so gladly and without shame. He had no idea she loved him. How much sharing these past few weeks had meant to her.

And then he jerked his mouth away and quickly removed his boots. Afterward, he carried her into the office and stood her by the desk as he began taking off her clothes with a frenzy that had her head spinning. One part of her wanted to tell him to slow down and to assure him she wasn't going anywhere. But another part was just as eager and excited as he was to get naked, and kept insisting that he hurry up.

Within minutes, more like seconds, spooned between

his body and the desk, she was totally naked. The cool air from the air conditioner that swept across her heated skin made her want to cover herself with her hands, but he wouldn't let her. He gently grabbed her wrists in his and held them up over her head, which made her breasts tilt up in perfect alignment to his lips when he leaned down.

On a breathless sigh he eased a nipple into his mouth, sucking it in between his lips and then licking the throbbing tip. She arched her back, felt him gently ease her onto the desk and realized he was practically on the desk with her. The metal surface felt cool to her back, but the warmth of his body felt hot to her front.

He lowered his hand to her sex and the stroke of his fingers on the folds of her labia made her groan out sounds she'd never made before. She'd thought from the first that he had skillful fingers and they were thrumming through her, stirring all kinds of sensations within her. Their lovemaking would often range from gentle to hard and she knew today would be one of those hard times. For whatever reason, he was driven to take her now, without any gentleness of any kind. He was stroking a need within her that wanted it just as fast and hard as he could deliver.

He took a step back and quickly removed his jeans and boxers. When she saw him—in his engorged splendor—a sound of dire need erupted from deep within her throat. He was bringing her to this, this intense state of want and need that was fueled by passion and desire.

"I want to know your taste, baby."

It was on the tip of her tongue to say that as many times as he'd made a meal out of her that he should know it pretty well by now. Instead when he crouched down in front of her body, which was all but spread out on the desk, and proceeded to wrap her legs over his shoulders, she automatically arched her back.

And when she felt his hot mouth close in on her sex, slide his tongue through her womanly folds, she lifted her hips off the table with the intimate contact. And when he began suckling hard, using his tongue to both torture and pleasure, she let out an intense moan as an orgasm tore through her body; sensations started at the soles of her feet and traveled like wildfire all the way to the crown of her head. And then she screamed at the top of her lungs.

Shudders continued to rip through her, made her muscles both ache and rejuvenate. And she couldn't help but lie there while Jason continued to get the taste he wanted.

When her shudders finally subsided, he gave her body one complete and thorough lick before lifting his head and looking up at her with a satisfied smile on his face, and the way he began licking his lips made her feel hot all over again.

He reached out and spread her legs wide and began stroking her again and she began moaning at the contact. "My fingers are all wet, which means you're ready," he said. "Now for me to get ready."

And she knew without looking that he was tearing into a condom packet and soon would be sliding the latex over his erection. After that first time in the hotel he'd never made love to her unprotected again, which gave her even more reason to think he wasn't ready for children. At least not with her, anyway.

From the feel of his erection pressing against her thigh she would definitely agree that at least he was ready for this, probably more ready than any man had a right to be, but she had no complaints.

She came to full attention when she felt his swollen, engorged member easing between her legs, and when he centered it to begin sliding between the folds of her labia and then suddenly thrust forward without any preamble, she began shuddering all over again.

"Look at me, baby. I want to be looking in your eyes when you come. I need to see it happen, Bella."

She looked up and met his gaze. He was buried deep inside of her and then holding tight to her gaze, he began moving, holding tight to the hips whose legs were wrapped firmly around him. They began moving together seemingly in perfect rhythm, faultless harmony and seamless precision. With each deep and thorough stroke, she felt all of him…every glorious inch.

"You tasted good and now you feel good," he said in a guttural voice while holding steadfast to her gaze. "Do you have any idea how wonderful you are making me feel?"

She had an idea. If it was anything close to how he was making her feel then the feelings were definitely mutual. And to show him just how mutual, her inner muscles began clamping down on him, milking him. She could tell from the look in his eyes the exact moment he realized what she was doing and the effect it was having on him. The more she milked him the bigger he seemed to get inside of her, as if he intended for her to have it all.

Today she felt greedy and was glad he intended to supply her needs. She dug her nails into his shoulders, at the moment not caring if she was branding him for life. And then he picked up the tempo and pleasure, the likes of nothing she'd experienced before dimming her vision. But through it all, she kept her gaze locked on his and saw how every sound, every move she made, got to him and triggered him to keep it coming.

And then when she felt her body break into fragments, she screamed out his name and he began pumping into her as if his very life depended on it. The orgasm that ripped through her snatched the breath from her lungs as his intense, relentless strokes almost drove her over the edge. And when she heard the hoarse cry from his own lips, saw the flash of something dark and turbulent in the depths of his eyes, she lost it and screamed again at the top of her lungs as another orgasm shook the core of everything inside her body.

And he followed her, pushed over the edge, while he continued to thrust even deeper. He buried his fingers into her hair and leaned down and captured her mouth to kiss the trembles right off her lips. At that moment she wished she could say all the words that had formed in her heart, words of love she wanted him to know. But she couldn't. This was all there was between them. She had accepted that long ago. And for the moment she was satisfied and content.

And when the day came that he wanted her gone, memories like these would sustain her, get her through each day without him.

And she prayed to God the memories would be enough.

"So when can we plan your wedding reception?" Megan asked when the Westmorelands had assembled around the dinner table at Dillon's place a few weeks later.

When Bella didn't say anything but looked over at Jason, he shrugged and said, "Throw some dates out to see if they will work for us."

Megan began rambling off dates, saying the first weekend in August would be perfect since all the Westmorelands away at college would be home and Micah, who was presently in Beijing, had sent word he would be back in the States during that time, as well. Gemma, who was expecting, had gotten the doctor's okay to travel from Australia then.

"And," Megan continued, "I spoke with Casey yesterday and she's checked with the other Westmorelands and that will give them plenty of time to make plans to be here, as well. I'm so excited."

Jason glanced over at Bella again thinking he was glad someone was. There was something going on with his wife that he just couldn't put a finger on and whatever it was had put him at a disadvantage. He knew she was upset with the outcome of the Bostwick twins. With all the evidence mounted against the twins, their attorney had convinced their parents to enter a guilty plea in hopes they would get a lesser sentence.

However, given prior mischievous pranks that had gotten the pair into trouble with the law before, the judge was not all that lenient and gave them two years. Bella had insisted on going to the sentencing hearing and he'd warned her against it but she'd been adamant. Things hadn't gone well when Kenneth, who still refused to accept blame for his part in any of it, made a scene, accusing Bella as the one responsible for what had happened to his grandsons. Since that day Jason had noted a change in her and she'd begun withdrawing from him. He'd tried getting her to talk, but she refused to do so.

"So what do the two of you think?" Megan asked, drawing his attention again.

He glanced at Bella. "What do you think, sweetheart?"

She placed a smile on her lips that he knew was forced. "That time is fine with me, but I doubt Mom and Dad will come either way."

"Then they will miss a good party," Jason replied. He then turned to Megan. "The first weekend in August is fine."

Later, on the ride back to their place, Jason finally found out what was troubling Bella. "I rode over to my ranch today, Jason. Why didn't you tell me work hadn't begun on the house yet?"

"There was no reason to tell you. You knew I was taking care of things, didn't you?"

"Yes. But I assumed work had gotten started already."

"I saw no reason to begin work on the place yet, given we're having a lot of rainy days around here now. It's not a good time to start any type of construction. Besides, it's not like you're going to move into the house or anything."

"You don't know that."

He had pulled into the yard and brought the truck to a stop and turned the ignition off. He glanced over at her. "I don't? I thought I did."

He tilted his hat back from his eyes and stared over at her. "Why would you need to move back into the house?"

Instead of holding his gaze she glanced out the window and looked ahead at his house, which he now considered as their house. "Our marriage is only supposed to last a year and I'm going to need somewhere to live when it ends."

Her words were like a kick in the gut. She was already

planning for the time when she would be leaving him? Why? He thought things were going great between them. "What's going on, Bella?"

"Nothing is going on. I just need to be realistic and remember that although we enjoy being bed partners, the reason we married stemmed from your proposal, which I accepted knowing full well the terms. And they are terms we must not forget."

Jason simply looked at her as he swore under his breath. She thought the only thing between them was the fact they were bed partners? "Thanks for reminding me, Bella." He then got out of the truck.

That was the first night they slept in the same bed but didn't make love and Bella lay there hurting inside and wasn't sure what she could do about it. She was trying to protect her heart, especially after the results of the pregnancy test she'd taken a few days ago.

Jason was an honorable man. Just the kind of man who'd keep her around just because she was the mother of his child. She wasn't particularly thinking of herself per se but of her child. She had grown up in a loveless household and simply refused to subject her child to one. Jason would never understand how that could be because he'd grown up with parents who'd loved each other and had set a good example for their children to follow. That was evident in the way his cousins and brother treated the wives they loved. It was easy to see their relationships were loving ones, the kinds that last until death. She didn't expect that kind of long-term commitment from Jason. That was not in the plan and had not been in his proposal.

She knew he was awake by the sound of his breathing but his back was to her as hers was to him. When he had come up to bed he hadn't said anything. In fact he had barely cast a glance her way before sliding under the covers.

His family was excited about hosting a wedding reception for them but she had been tempted to tell them not to bother. Their year would be up before she knew it anyway. However, she had sat there and listened while plans were being made and fighting the urge to get pulled into the excitement.

The bed shifted and she held her breath hoping that, although she'd given him that reminder, he would still want her. He dashed that hope when instead of sliding toward her he got out of the bed and left the room. Was he coming back to bed or did he plan on sleeping somewhere else tonight? On the sofa? In his truck?

She couldn't help the tears that begin falling from her eyes. She only had herself to blame. No one told her to fall in love. She should have known better. She should not have put her heart out there. But she had and now she was paying the price for doing so.

"Okay, what the hell is wrong with you, Jason? It's not like you to make such a stupid mistake and the one you just made was a doozy," Zane stormed. "That's the sheikh's prized horse and what you did could have cost him a leg."

Anger flared up inside of Jason. "Dammit, Zane, I know what I did. You don't have to remind me."

He then glanced over at Derringer and waited to see what he had to say and when he didn't say anything, Jason was grateful.

"Look, guys, I'm sorry about the mistake. I've got a lot on my mind. I think I'll call it a day before I cause another major screwup." He then walked off toward Zane's barn.

He was in the middle of saddling his horse to leave when Derringer walked up. "Hey, man, you want to talk about it?"

Jason drew in a deep breath. "No."

"Come on, Jas, there's evidently trouble in paradise at Jason's Place. I don't profess to be an expert when it comes to such matters, but even you will admit that me and Lucia had a number of clashes before we married."

Jason glanced over at him. "What about *after* you married?"

Derringer threw his head back and laughed. "Want a list? The main thing to remember is the two of you are people with different personalities and that in itself is bound to cause problems. The most effective solution is good, open communication. We talk it out and then we make love. Works every time. Oh, and you need to remind her every so often how much you love her."

Jason chuckled dryly. "The first two things you said I should do are things I can handle but not the latter."

Derringer raised a brow. "What? You can't tell your wife you love her?"

Jason sighed. "No, I can't tell her."

Derringer looked confused. "Why? You do love her, don't you?"

"Yes, more than life."

"Then what's the problem?"

Jason stopped what he was doing and met Derringer's gaze. "She doesn't love me back."

Derringer blinked and then drew back slightly and said, "Of course she loves you."

Jason shook his head. "No, she doesn't." He paused

for a moment and then said, "Our marriage was based on a business proposition, Derringer. She needed a husband to retain her trust fund and I wanted her land—at least co-ownership of her land—and Hercules."

Derringer stared at him for a long moment and then said, "I think you'd better start from the beginning."

It took Jason less than ten minutes to tell Derringer everything, basically because his cousin stood there and listened without asking any questions. But once he'd finished the questions had begun…as well as the observations.

Derringer was certain Bella loved him because he claimed she looked at Jason the way Lucia looked at him, the way Chloe looked at Ramsey and the way Pam looked at Dillon—when they thought no one was supposed to be watching.

Then Derringer claimed that given the fact Jason and Bella were still sharing the same bed—although no hanky-panky had been going on for almost a week now—had significant meaning.

Jason shook his head. "If Bella loves me the way you think she does then why hasn't she told me?"

Derringer crossed his arms over his chest. "And why haven't you told her?" When Jason couldn't answer Derringer smiled and said, "I think the two of you have a big communication problem. It happens and is something that can easily be corrected."

Jason couldn't help but smile. "Sounds like you've gotten to be a real expert on the subject of marriage."

Derringer chuckled. "I have to be. I plan on being a married man for life so I need to know what it takes to keep my woman happy and to understand that when wifey isn't happy, hubby's life can be a living hell."

Derringer then tapped his foot on the barn's wooden floor as if he was trying to make up his mind about something. "I really shouldn't be telling you this because it's something I overheard Chloe and Lucia discussing yesterday and if Lucia found out I was eavesdropping she—"

"What?"

"Maybe you already know but just hadn't mentioned anything."

"Dammit, Derringer, what the hell are you talking about?"

A sly smile eased across Derringer's lips. "The ladies in the family suspect Bella might be pregnant."

Bella walked out of the children's hospital with a smile on her face. She loved kids and being around them always made her forget her troubles, which was why she would come here a couple of days a week to spend time with them. She glanced at her watch. It was still early yet and she wasn't ready to go home.

Home.

She couldn't help but think of Jason's Place as her home. Although she'd made a stink with Jason about construction on her ranch, she didn't relish the thought of going back there to live. She had gotten accustomed to her home with Jason.

She was more confused than ever and the phone call from her mother hadn't helped. Now her parents were trying to work out a bargain with her—another proposal of a sort. They would have their attorney draw up a legal document that stated if she returned home they would give her the space she needed. Of course they wanted her to move back onto their estate, although she would be given the entire east wing as her own. They claimed they no longer wanted to control her life, but just wanted to make sure she was living the kind of life she was entitled to live.

Their proposal sounded good but she had gotten into enough trouble accepting proposals already. Besides, even if things didn't work out between her and Jason, he deserved to be around his child. When they divorced, at least his son or daughter would be a stone's throw away.

She was crossing the parking lot to her car when she heard someone call her name. She turned and cringed when she saw it was her uncle Kenneth's daughter, who was the mother of the twins. Although Uncle Kenneth had had an outburst at the trial, Elyse Bostwick Thomas had not. She'd been too busy crying.

Drawing in a deep breath Bella waited for the woman to catch up with her. "Elyse."

"Bella. I just wanted to say how sorry I was for what Mark and Michael did. I know Dad is still bitter and I've tried talking to him about it but he refuses to discuss it. He's always spoiled the boys and there was nothing I could do about it, mainly because my husband and I are divorced. My ex moved away, but I wanted a father figure in their lives."

Elyse didn't say anything for a moment. "I hope Dad will eventually realize his part in all this, and although I miss my sons, they were getting too out of hand. I've been assured the place they are going will teach them discipline. I just wanted you to know I was wrong for listening to everything Dad said about you and when I found out you even offered to help pay for my sons' attorney I thought that was generous of you."

Bella nodded. "Uncle Kenneth turned down my offer."

"Yes, but just the thought touched me deeply considering everything. You and I are family and I hope that one day we can be friends."

A smile touched Bella's lips. "I'd like that, Elyse. I really would."

"Bella, are you sure you're okay? You might want to go see the doctor about that stomach virus."

Bella glanced over at Chloe. On her way home she had dropped by to visit with her cousin-in-law and little Susan. Bella had grown fond of the baby who was a replica of both of her parents. The little girl had Ramsey's eyes and skin tone and Chloe's mouth and nose. "Yes, Chloe, I'm fine."

She decided not to say anything about her pregnancy just yet until after she figured out how and when she would tell Jason. Evidently Chloe had gotten suspicious because Bella had thrown up the other day when Chloe had come to deliver a package to Jason from Ramsey.

Bella knew from the bits and pieces of the stories she'd heard from the ladies that Chloe was pregnant when she and Ramsey had married. However, Bella doubted that was the reason Ramsey had married her. Anyone around the pair for any period of time could tell how in love they were.

Bella never had a best friend, no other woman to share her innermost feminine secrets with. That was one of the reasons she appreciated the bond she felt toward all the Westmoreland women. They were all friendly, understanding and supportive. But she was hoping that because Chloe had been pregnant when she'd married Ramsey, her in-law could help her understand a few things. She had decisions to make that would impact her baby's future.

"Chloe, can I ask you something?"

Chloe smiled over at her. "Sure."

"When you found out you were pregnant were you afraid to tell Ramsey for fear of how he would react?"

Chloe placed her teacup down on the table and her smile brightened as if she was recalling that time. "I didn't discover I was pregnant until Ramsey and I broke up. But the one thing I knew was that I was going to tell him because he had every right to know. The one thing that I wasn't sure about was when I was going to tell him. One time I thought of taking the coward's way out and waiting until I returned to Florida and calling him from there."

Chloe paused for a moment and then said, "Ramsey made things easy for me when he came to me. We patched up things between us, found it had been nothing more than a huge misunderstanding and got back together. It was then that I told him about my pregnancy and he was happy about it."

Bella took a sip of her tea and then asked, "When the two of you broke up did you stay apart for long?"

"For over three weeks and they were the unhappiest three weeks of my life." Chloe smiled again when she added, "A Westmoreland man has a tendency to grow on you, Bella. They become habit-forming. And when it comes to babies, they love them."

There was no doubt in Bella's mind that Jason loved children; that wasn't what worried her. The big question was if he'd want to father any with her considering the nature of their marriage. Would he see that as a noose around his neck? For all she knew he might be counting the days until their year would be up so he could go his way and she go hers. A baby would definitely change things.

She glanced back over at Chloe. "Ramsey is a wonderful father."

Chloe smiled. "Yes, and Jason would be a wonderful father, as well. When their parents died all the Westmorelands had to pitch in and raise the younger ones. It was a team effort and it wasn't easy. Jason is wonderful with children and would make any child a fantastic father."

Chloe chuckled. "I can see him with a son while teaching him to ride his first pony, or a daughter who will wrap him around her finger the way Susan does Ramsey. I can see you and Jason having a houseful of kids."

Bella nodded. Chloe could only see that because she thought she and Jason had a normal marriage.

"Don't ever underestimate a Westmoreland man, Bella."

Chloe's words interrupted her thoughts. "What do you mean?"

"I mean that from what I've discovered in talking with all the other wives, even those spread out in Montana, Texas, Atlanta and Charlotte, a Westmoreland man is loyal and dedicated to a fault to the woman he's chosen as a mate. The woman he loves. And although they can be overly protective at times, you can't find a man more loving and supportive. But the one thing they don't care too much for is when we hold secrets from them. Secrets that need to be shared with them. Jason is special, and I believe the longer you and he are married, the more you will see just how special he is."

Chloe reached out and gently touched Bella's hand. "I hope what I've said has helped in some way."

Bella returned her smile. "It has." Bella knew that

she needed to tell Jason about the baby. And whatever decision he made regarding their future, she would have to live with it.

Ten

Jason didn't bother riding his horse back home after his discussion with Derringer. Instead he borrowed Zane's truck and drove home like a madman only to discover Bella wasn't there. She hadn't mentioned anything at breakfast about going out, so where was she? But then they hadn't been real chatty lately, so he wasn't really surprised she hadn't told him anything.

He glanced around his home—their home—and took in the changes she'd made. Subtle changes but changes he liked. If she were to leave his house—their house—it wouldn't be the same. He wouldn't be the same.

He drew in a deep breath. What if the ladies' suspicions were true and she was pregnant? What if Derringer's suspicions were true and she loved him? Hell, if both suspicions were true then they had one hell of a major communication problem between them, and it was one he intended to remedy today as soon as she returned.

He walked into the kitchen and began making of all things, a cup of tea. Jeez, Bella had definitely rubbed off on him but he wouldn't have it any other way. And what if she was really pregnant? The thought of her stomach growing big while she carried his child almost left him breathless. And he could recall when it happened.

It had to have been their wedding night spent in the honeymoon suite of the Four Seasons. He had awakened to find her mouth on him and she had driven him to more passion than he'd ever felt in his entire life. He'd ended up flipping her on her back and taking her without wearing a condom. He had exploded the moment he'd gotten inside her body. Evidently she had been good and fertile that night.

He certainly hoped so. The thought of her having his baby was his most fervent desire. And no matter what she thought, he would provide both her and his child with a loving home.

He heard the sound of the front door opening and paused a moment not to rush out and greet her. They needed to talk and he needed to create a comfortable environment for them to do so. He was determined that before they went to bed tonight there would be a greater degree of understanding between them. With that resolution, he placed the teacup on the counter to go greet his wife.

Bella's grooming and social training skills had prepared her to handle just about anything, but now that she was back at Jason's Place she was no longer sure of her capabilities. So much for all the money her parents had poured into those private schools.

She placed her purse on the table thinking at least she'd had one bright spot in her day other than the time spent with the kids. And that was her discussion with Elyse. They had made plans to get together for tea later in the week. She could just imagine how her uncle would handle it when he found out she and Elyse had decided to be friends.

And then there had been her conversation with Chloe. It had definitely been an eye-opener and made her realize she couldn't keep her secret from Jason any longer. He deserved to know about the baby and she would tell him tonight.

"Bella. You're home."

She was pulled from her reverie by the pure masculine tone of Jason's voice when he walked out of the kitchen. Her pulse hammered in the center of her throat and she wondered if he would always have this kind of effect on her. She took a second or two to compose herself, before she responded to him. "Yes, I'm home. I see you have company."

He lifted a brow. "Company?"

"Yes. Zane's truck is parked outside," she replied, allowing her gaze to roam over her husband, unable to stop herself from doing so. He was such a hunk and no matter what he wore it only enhanced his masculinity. Even the jeans and chambray shirt he was wearing now made him look sexy as hell.

"I borrowed it. He's not here."

"Oh." That meant they were alone. Under the same roof. And hadn't made love in almost a week. So it stood to reason that the deep vibrations of his voice would stir across her skin and that turn-you-on mouth of his would make her panties start to feel damp.

She met his gaze and something akin to potent sexual awareness passed between them, charging the air, electrifying the moment. She felt it and was sure he felt it, as well. She studied his features and knew she wanted a son or daughter who looked just like him.

She knew she needed to break into the sensual vibe surrounding them and go up the stairs, or else she would be tempted to do something crazy like cross the room and throw herself in his arms and beg him to want her, to love her, to want the child they had conceived together.

"Well, I guess I'll go upstairs a moment and—"

"Do you have a moment so we can talk, Bella?"

She swallowed deeply. "Talk?"

"Yes."

That meant she was going to have to sit across from him and watch that sensual mouth of his move, see his tongue work and remember what it felt like dueling nonstop with hers and—

"Bella, could we talk?"

She swallowed again. "Now?"

"Yes."

"Sure," she murmured and then she followed him toward the kitchen. Studying his backside she could only think that the man she had married was such a hottie.

Jason wasn't sure where they needed to begin but he did know they needed to begin somewhere.

"I was about to have a cup of tea. Would you like a cup, as well?"

He wondered if she recalled those were the exact words she had spoken to him that first time she had invited him inside her house. They were words he still remembered to this day. And from the trace of amusement that touched her lips, he knew that she had recalled them.

"Yes, I'd love a cup. Thank you," she said, sitting down at the table, unintentionally flashing a bit of thigh.

He stepped back and quickly moved to the counter, trying to fight for control and to not remember this is the woman whom he'd given her first orgasm, the woman who'd awakened him one morning with her mouth on him, the first woman he'd had unprotected sex with, the only woman he'd wanted to shoot his release inside of, but more than anything, this was the woman he loved so very much.

Moments later when he turned back to her with cups of tea in his hands, he could tell she was nervous, was probably wondering what he wanted to talk about and was hoping he would hurry and get it over with.

"So, how was your day today?" he asked, sitting across from her at the table.

She shrugged those delicate shoulders he liked running his tongue over. She looked so sinfully sexy in the sundress she was wearing. "It was nice. I spent a lot of it at the children's hospital. Today was 'read-a-story' day and I entertained a bunch of them. I had so much fun."

"I'm glad."

"I also ran into Uncle Kenneth's daughter, Elyse."

"The mother of the twins, right?"

"Yes."

"And how did that go?" Jason asked.

"Better than I expected. Unlike Uncle Kenneth, she's not holding me responsible for what happened to her sons. She says they were getting out of hand anyway and is hoping the two years will teach them discipline," Bella said.

"We can all hope for that" was Jason's response.

"Yes, but in a way I feel sorry for her. I can only imagine how things were for her having Kenneth for a father. My dad wouldn't get a 'Father of the Year' trophy, either, but at least I had friends I met at all those schools they shipped me off to. It never bothered me when I didn't go home for the holidays. It helped when I went home with friends and saw how parents were supposed to act. Not as business partners but as human beings."

Bella realized after she'd said it that in a way Jason was her business partner, but she'd never thought of him that way. From the time he'd slipped a ring on her finger she had thought of him as her husband—for better or worse.

The kitchen got silent as they sipped tea.

"So what do you want to talk about, Jason?"

Good question, Jason thought. "I want to talk about us."

He saw her swallow. "Us?"

"Yes, us. Lately, I haven't been feeling an 'us' and I want to ask you a question."

She glanced over at him. "What?"

"Do you not want to be married to me anymore?"

She broke eye contact with him to study the pattern design on her teacup. "What gave you that idea?"

"Want a list?"

She shot her gaze back to him. "I didn't think you'd notice."

"Is that what this is about, Bella, me not noticing you, giving you attention?"

She quickly shook her head. Heaven help her or him if he were to notice her any more or give her more attention than she was already getting. To say Jason Westmoreland was all into her was an understatement.

Unfortunately he was all into her, literally. And all for the wrong reasons. Sex was great but it couldn't hold a marriage together. It couldn't replace love no matter how many orgasms you had a night.

"Bella?"

"No, that's not it," she said, nervously biting her bottom lip.

"Then what is it, sweetheart? What do you need that I'm not giving you? What can I do to make you happy? I need to know because your leaving me is not an option. I love you too much to let you go."

The teacup froze midway to her lips. She stared over at him in shock. "What did you just say?"

"A number of things. Do I need to repeat it all?"

She shook her head, putting her cup down. "No, just the last part."

"About me loving you?"

"Yes."

"I said I loved you too much to let you go. Lately you've been reminding me about the year I mentioned in my proposal, but there isn't a year time frame, Bella. I threw that in as an adjustment period to not scare you off. I never intended to end things between us."

He saw the single tear flow from her eyes. "You didn't?"

"No. I love you too much to let you go. There, I've said it again and I will keep saying it until you finally hear it. Believe it. Accept it."

"I didn't know you loved me, Jason. I love you, too. I think I fell in love with you the first time I saw you at your family's charity ball."

"And that's when I believe I fell in love with you, as well," he said, pushing the chair back to get up from the table. "I knew there was a reason every time we touched a part of my soul would stir, my heart would melt and my desire for you would increase."

"I thought it was all about sex."

"No. I believe the reason the sex between us was so good, so damn hot, was that it was fueled by love of the most intense kind. More than once I wanted to tell you I loved you but I wasn't sure you were ready to hear it. I didn't want to run you off."

"And knowing you loved me is what I needed to hear," she said, standing. "I've never thought I could be loved and I wanted so much for you to love me."

"Sweetheart, I do. I love every single thing about you."

"Oh, Jason."

She went to him and was immediately swept up into his arms, held tight. And when he lowered his head to kiss her, her mouth was ready, willing and hungry. That was evident in the way her tongue mated with his with such intensity.

Moments later he pulled back and swept her off her feet and into his arms then walked out of the kitchen.

Somehow they made it upstairs to the bedroom. And there in the middle of the room, he kissed Bella again with a hunger that she greedily returned. He finally released her mouth to draw in a deep breath, but before she could draw in one of her own, he flipped her dress up to her waist and was pulling a pair of wet panties down her thighs. She barely had time to react before he moved to her hips to bury his head between her legs.

"Jason!"

She came the moment his tongue whipped inside of her and began stroking her labia, but she quickly saw that wouldn't be enough for him. He sharpened the tip of his tongue and literally stabbed deep inside of her and proceeded to lick circles around her clitoris before drawing it in between his lips.

Her eyes fluttered closed as he then began suckling her senseless as desire, more potent than any she'd ever felt, started consuming her, racing through every part of her body and pushing her toward a orgasm.

"Jason!"

And he still didn't let up. She reached for him but couldn't get a firm hold as his tongue began thrusting inside her again. His tongue, she thought, should be patented with a warning sign. Whenever he parted this life it should be donated to the Smithsonian.

And when she came yet again, he spread her thighs wide to lap her up. She moaned deep in her throat as his tongue and lips made a plaything of her clitoris, driving her demented, crazy with lust, when sensations after earth-shattering sensations rammed through her.

And then suddenly he pulled back and through glazed eyes she watched as he stood and quickly undressed himself and then proceeded to undress her, as well. Her gaze went to his erection.

Without further ado, he carried her over to the bed, placed her on her back, slid over her and settled between her legs and aimed his shaft straight toward the damp folds of her labia.

"Yes!" she almost screamed out, and then she felt him, pushing inside her, desperate to be joined with her.

He stopped moving. Dropped his head down near hers and said in a sensual growl, "No condom tonight."

Bella gazed up at him. "No condom tonight or any other night for a while," she whispered. "I'll tell you why later. It's something I planned to tell you tonight anyway." And before she could dwell too much on just what she had to tell him, he began thrusting inside of her.

And when he pushed all the way to the hilt she gasped for breath at the fullness of having him buried so deep inside her. Her muscles clung to him, she was holding him tight and she began massaging him, milking his shaft for everything she had and thought she could get, while thinking a week had been too long.

He widened her legs farther with his hands and lifted her hips to drive deeper still and she almost cried when he began a steady thrusting inside of her, with relentless precision. This was the kind of ecstasy she'd missed. She hadn't known such degrees of pleasure existed until him and when he lifted her legs onto his shoulders while thrusting back and forth inside her, their gazes met through dazed lashes.

"Come for me, baby," he whispered. "Come for me now."

Her body complied and began to shudder in a climax so gigantic she felt the house shaking. She screamed. There was no way she could not, and when he began coming inside her, his hot release thickened by the intensity of their lovemaking, she could only cry out as she was swept away yet again.

And then he leaned up and kissed her, but not before whispering that he loved her and that he planned to spend the rest of his life making her happy, making her feel loved. And she believed him.

With all the strength she could muster, she leaned up to meet him.

"And I love you so very much, too."

And she meant it.

"Why don't I have to wear a condom for a while?" Jason asked moments later with her entwined in his arms, their limbs tangled as they enjoyed the aftermath of their lovemaking together. He knew the reason, but he wanted her to confirm it.

She lifted her head slightly, met his gaze and whispered, "I'm having your baby."

Her announcement did something to him. Being given confirmation that a life they had created together was growing inside her made him shudder. He knew she was waiting for him to say something.

He planned to show her he had taken it well. She needed to know just how happy her announcement had made him. "Knowing that you are pregnant with my child, Bella, is the greatest gift I could ever hope to receive."

"Oh, Jason."

And then she was there, closer into his arms with her arms wrapped around his neck. "I was afraid you wouldn't be happy."

"You were afraid for nothing. I am ecstatic, overjoyed at the prospect of being a father. Thank you for everything you've done, all the happiness you've brought me."

She shook her head. "No, it's I who needs to thank you for sharing your family with me, for giving me your support when my own family tried to break me down. And for loving me."

And then she leaned toward his lips and he gave her what she wanted, what he wanted. He knew at that moment the proposal had worked. It had brought them together in a way they thought wasn't possible. And he would always appreciate and be forever thankful that Bella had come into his life.

Two days later the Westmorelands met at Dillon's for breakfast to celebrate. It seemed everyone had announcements to make and Dillon felt it was best that they were all made at the same time so they could all rejoice and celebrate.

First Dillon announced he'd received word from Bane that he would be graduating from the naval academy in a few months with honors. Dillon almost choked up when he'd said it, which let everyone know the magnitude of Bane's accomplishments in the eyes of his family. They knew Bane's first year in the navy had been hard since he hadn't known the meaning of discipline. But he'd finally straightened up and had dreams of becoming a SEAL. He'd worked hard and found favor with one of the high-ranking chief petty officers who'd recognized his potential and recommended him for the academy.

Zane then announced that Hercules had done his duty and had impregnated Silver Fly and everyone could only anticipate the beauty of the foal she would one day deliver.

Ramsey followed and said he'd received word from Storm Westmoreland that his wife, Jayla, was expecting and so were Durango and his wife, Savannah. Reggie and Libby's twins were now crawling all over the place. And then with a huge smile on his face Ramsey announced that he and Chloe were having another baby. That sent out loud cheers and it seemed the loudest had come from Chloe's father, Senator Jamison Burton of Florida, who along with Chloe's stepmother, had arrived the day before to visit with his daughter, son-in-law and granddaughter.

Everyone got quiet when Jason stood to announce that he and Bella would be having a baby in the spring, as well. Bella's eyes were glued to Jason as he spoke and she could feel the love radiating from his every word.

"Bella and I are converting her grandfather's ranch into a guest house and combining our lands for our future children to enjoy one day," he ended by saying.

"Does that mean the two of you want more than one child?" Zane asked with a sly chuckle.

Jason glanced over at Bella. "Yes, I want as many children as my wife wants to give me. We can handle it, can't we, sweetheart?"

Bella smiled. "Yes, we can handle it." And they would because what had started out as a proposal had ended up being a whole lot more and she was filled with overflowing joy at how Jason and his family had enriched her life.

He reached out his hand to her and she took it. Hers felt comforting in his and she could only be thankful for her Westmoreland man.

Epilogue

"When I first heard you'd gotten married I wondered about the quickness of it, Jason, but after meeting Bella I understand why," Micah said to his brother. "She's beautiful."

"Thanks." Jason smiled as he glanced around the huge guest house on his and Bella's property. The weather had cooperated and the construction workers had been able to transform what had once been a ranch house into a huge fifteen room guest house for family, friends and business associates of the Westmorelands. Combining the old with the new, the builder and his crew had done a fantastic job and Jason and Bella couldn't be more pleased.

He glanced across the way and saw Dillon was talking to Bane who'd surprised everyone by showing up. It was the first time he'd returned home since he had left nearly three years ago. Jason had gotten the chance to have a long conversation with his youngest brother. He was not the bad-assed kid of yesteryears but standing beside Dillon in his naval officer's uniform, the family couldn't be more proud of the man he had become. But there still was that pain behind the sharpness of Bane's eyes. Although he hadn't mentioned Crystal's name, everyone in the family knew the young woman who'd been Bane's first love, his fixation probably since puberty, was still in his thoughts and probably had a permanent place in his heart. He could only imagine the conversation Dillon was having with Bane since they both had intense expressions on their faces.

"So you've not given up on Crystal?" Dillon asked his youngest brother.

Bane shook his head. "No. A man can never give up on the woman he loves. She's in my blood and I believe that no matter where she is, I'm in hers." Bane paused a moment. "But that's the crux of my problem. I have no idea where she is."

Bane then studied Dillon's features. "And you're sure that you don't?"

Dillon inhaled deeply. "Yes, I'm being honest with you, Bane. When the Newsomes moved away they didn't leave anyone a forwarding address. I just think they wanted to put as much distance between you and them as possible. But I'll still go on record and say that I think the time apart for you and Crystal was a good thing. She was young and so were you. The two of you were headed for trouble and both of you needed to grow up. I am proud of the man you've become."

"Thanks, but one day when I have a lot of time I'm going to find her, Dillon, and nobody, her parents or anyone, will keep me from claiming what's mine."

Dillon saw the intense look in Bane's face and only

hoped that wherever Crystal Newsome was that she loved Bane just as much as Bane still loved her.

Jason glanced over at Bella who was talking to her parents. The Bostwicks had surprised everyone by flying in for the reception. So far they'd been on their good behavior, probably because they were still in awe by the fact that Jason was related to Thorn Westmoreland—racing legend; Stone Westmoreland—aka Rock Mason, *New York Times* bestselling author; Jared Westmoreland, whose reputation as a divorce attorney was renowned; Senator Reggie Westmoreland, and that Dillon was the CEO of Blue Ridge. Hell, they were even speechless when they learned there was even a sheikh in the family.

He saw that Bella was pretending to hang on to her parents' every word. He had discovered she knew how to handle them and refused to let them treat her like a child. He hadn't had to step in once to put them in their place. Bella had managed to do that rather nicely on her own. They had opted to stay at a hotel in town, which had been fine with both him and Bella. There was only so much of her parents that either of them could take.

He inwardly smiled as he studied Bella's features and could tell she was ready to be rescued. "Excuse me a minute, Micah, I need to go claim my wife for a second." Jason moved across the yard to her and as if she felt his impending presence, she glanced his way and smiled. She then excused herself from her parents and headed to meet him.

The dress she was wearing was beautiful and the style hid the little pooch of her stomach. The doctor had warned them that because of the way her stomach was growing they shouldn't be surprised if she was having twins. It would be a couple of months before they knew for sure.

"Do you want to go somewhere for tea…and me," Jason leaned over to whisper close to her ear.

Bella smiled up at him. "Think we'll be missed?"

Jason chuckled. "With all these Westmorelands around, I doubt it. I don't even think your parents will miss us. Now they're standing over there hanging on to Sheikh Jamal Yasir's every word."

"I noticed."

Jason then took his wife's hand in his. "Come on. Let's take a stroll around our land."

And their land was beautiful, with the valley, the mountains, the blooming flowers and the lakes. Already he could envision a younger slew of Westmorelands that he and Bella would produce who would help take care of their land. They would love it as much as their parents did. Not for the first time he felt as if he was a blessed man, his riches abundant not in money or jewelry but in the woman walking by his side. His Southern Bella, his southern beauty, the woman that was everything to him and then some.

"I was thinking," he said.

She glanced over at him. "About what?"

He stopped walking and reached out and placed a hand on her stomach. "You, me and our baby."

She chuckled. "Our babies. Don't forget there is that possibility."

He smiled at the thought of that. "Yes, our babies. But mainly about the proposal."

She nodded. "What about it?"

"I suggest we do another."

She threw her head back and laughed. "I don't have any more land or another horse to bargain with."

"A moot point, Mrs. Westmoreland. This time the stakes will be higher."

"Mmm, what do you want?"

"Another baby pretty soon after this one."

She chuckled again. "Don't you know you never mention having more babies to a pregnant woman? But I'm glad to hear that you want a house filled with children because I do, too. You'll make a wonderful father."

"And you a beautiful mother."

And then he kissed her with all the love in his heart, sealing yet another proposal and knowing the woman he held in his arms would be the love of his life for always.

* * * * *

COMING NEXT MONTH

Available July 12, 2011

You can find more information on upcoming
Harlequin® titles, free excerpts and more at
www.HarlequinInsideRomance.com.

HDCNM0611

REQUEST YOUR FREE BOOKS!
2 FREE NOVELS PLUS 2 FREE GIFTS!

Harlequin®

Desire

ALWAYS POWERFUL, PASSIONATE AND PROVOCATIVE

YES! Please send me 2 FREE Harlequin Desire® novels and my 2 FREE gifts (gifts are worth about $10). After receiving them, if I don't wish to receive any more books, I can return the shipping statement marked "cancel." If I don't cancel, I will receive 6 brand-new novels every month and be billed just $4.05 per book in the U.S. or $4.74 per book in Canada. That's a saving of at least 15% off the cover price! It's quite a bargain! Shipping and handling is just 50¢ per book in the U.S. and 75¢ per book in Canada.* I understand that accepting the 2 free books and gifts places me under no obligation to buy anything. I can always return a shipment and cancel at any time. Even if I never buy another book, the two free books and gifts are mine to keep forever.

225/326 SDN FC65

Name _____ (PLEASE PRINT)

Address _____ Apt. #

City _____ State/Prov. _____ Zip/Postal Code

Signature (if under 18, a parent or guardian must sign)

Mail to the **Reader Service:**
IN U.S.A.: P.O. Box 1867, Buffalo, NY 14240-1867
IN CANADA: P.O. Box 609, Fort Erie, Ontario L2A 5X3

Not valid for current subscribers to Harlequin Desire books.

Want to try two free books from another line?
Call 1-800-873-8635 or visit www.ReaderService.com.

* Terms and prices subject to change without notice. Prices do not include applicable taxes. Sales tax applicable in N.Y. Canadian residents will be charged applicable taxes. Offer not valid in Quebec. This offer is limited to one order per household. All orders subject to credit approval. Credit or debit balances in a customer's account(s) may be offset by any other outstanding balance owed by or to the customer. Please allow 4 to 6 weeks for delivery. Offer available while quantities last.

Your Privacy—The Reader Service is committed to protecting your privacy. Our Privacy Policy is available online at www.ReaderService.com or upon request from the Reader Service.

We make a portion of our mailing list available to reputable third parties that offer products we believe may interest you. If you prefer that we not exchange your name with third parties, or if you wish to clarify or modify your communication preferences, please visit us at www.ReaderService.com/consumerschoice or write to us at Reader Service Preference Service, P.O. Box 9062, Buffalo, NY 14269. Include your complete name and address.

HDES11

USA TODAY *bestselling author B.J. Daniels takes you on a trip to Whitehorse, Montana, and the Chisholm Cattle Company.*

RUSTLED

Available July 2011 from Harlequin Intrigue.

As the dust settled, Dawson got his first good look at the rustler. A pair of big Montana sky-blue eyes glared up at him from a face framed by blond curls.

A woman rustler?

"You have to let me go," she hollered as the roar of the stampeding cattle died off in the distance.

"So you can finish stealing my cattle? I don't think so." Dawson jerked the woman to her feet.

She reached for the gun strapped to her hip hidden under her long barn jacket.

He grabbed the weapon before she could, his eyes narrowing as he assessed her. "How many others are there?" he demanded, grabbing a fistful of her jacket. "I think you'd better start talking before I tear into you."

She tried to fight him off, but he was on to her tricks and pinned her to the ground. He was suddenly aware of the soft curves beneath the jean jacket she wore under her coat.

"You have to listen to me." She ground out the words from between her gritted teeth. "You have to let me go. If you don't they will come back for me and they will kill you. There are too many of them for you to fight off alone. You won't stand a chance and I don't want your blood on my hands."

"I'm touched by your concern for me. Especially after you just tried to pull a gun on me."

"I wasn't going to shoot you."

Dawson hauled her to her feet and walked her the rest of the way to his horse. Reaching into his saddlebag, he pulled out a length of rope.

"You can't tie me up."

He pulled her hands behind her back and began to tie her wrists together.

"If you let me go, I can keep them from coming back," she said. "You have my word." She let out an unladylike curse. "I'm just trying to save your sorry neck."

"And I'm just going after my cattle."

"Don't you mean your boss's cattle?"

"Those cattle are mine."

"*You're* a Chisholm?"

"Dawson Chisholm. And you are…?"

"Everyone calls me Jinx."

He chuckled. "I can see why."

*Bronco busting, falling in love…it's all in a day's work.
Look for the rest of their story in*

RUSTLED

*Available July 2011 from Harlequin Intrigue
wherever books are sold.*

HIEXP0711R

THE NOTORIOUS
WOLFES

A powerful dynasty,
where secrets and scandal never sleep!

Eight siblings, blessed with wealth, but denied the one
thing they wanted—a father's love. Haunted by their
past and driven to succeed, the Wolfes scattered to the
far corners of the globe. It's said that even the blackest
of souls can be healed by the purest of love....

But can the dynasty rise again?